TILL THE RIVERS ALL RUN DRY

OTHER BOOKS BY JIM LESTER

FICTION

Fallout

The Great Pretender

NONFICTION

Greater Little Rock

Hoop Crazy: College Basketball in the 1950s

TILL THE RIVERS ALL RUN DRY

A Middle Grade Mystery/Adventure Novel

By

Jim Lester

Till the Rivers All Run Dry

Copyright © 2016 by Jim Lester

You may contact Jim Lester at info@JimLesterBooks.com.

This is a work of fiction. Names, characters, places, and incidents either are the product of the author's imagination or are used fictitiously, and any resemblance to actual persons, living or dead, events, or locales is entirely coincidental.

Cover by Mariposa Book Transformation Services
Edited by Helena Mariposa, Mariposa Book Transformation Services.

"Till the Rivers all run dry
Till the sun falls from the sky
Till life on earth is through
I'll be needing you."

"Till the Rivers All Run Dry"
—Wayland Holyfield

"How could God put our oil under their land?"

20th Century Bumper Sticker

« 1 »

One Friday evening right before the Fourth of July in the summer of 1941, I answered the front door and my whole life changed.

Two men in suits stood on the porch. One of them was an older fellow wearing a cheap brown suit and a high starched collar that was wilting from the summer heat. The band in his rumpled fedora was stained with sweat. He had a droopy mustache that was part black and part white and an Adam's apple that looked about the size of a baseball.

The other man was younger and had on a nicer suit. He removed his hat and showed off a thick head of blond hair. His face was pasty white, and I knew right off that he'd never done a lick of farmwork in his life.

"Is Mr. Chester Parker at home? We'd like a word with him if it would be convenient." The younger man sounded like Mr. Hunter who taught English over at El Dorado Junior High, where I had just finished the seventh grade. They both talked real educated and proper-like.

"I reckon he's out back," I said. "Y'all come on in and I'll get him." I looked past the two men on the porch and saw some angry-looking dark clouds gathering off to the east, promising a summer rain.

The two men stepped into the living room. The older man removed his hat and scratched his bald head.

Before I could fetch Daddy, Mama stepped into the living room from the kitchen. She was wearing her big red apron that was dusty with flour from making the biscuits for supper. She had a dot of flour on her nose. "Who is it, Ricky? Did you . . ." She pulled up short in the doorway and drew in a quick breath.

"Howdy, Dixie," the older man said. "How you been?"

Mama eyed the man like a dead garden snake she'd found on the back porch. "Evening, Mr. Taggert. I reckon I'm fine." Mama's tone filled the living room with a chilling frost.

The older man ignored Mama's coldness. "This here is Mr. George Quinn. He's from Washington. We need to have a word with Mr. Ches if we might."

I couldn't believe what I was hearing. Washington? What on earth would some stranger from Washington, DC, want with my father?

Mama wiped her hands on her apron. "Ricky, run on out to the shed and fetch your daddy. Be quick now."

I scampered back through the kitchen and out the screen door and sprinted across the yard to the shed. I found Daddy hunched over his worktable lost in thought, staring at the parts of a radio he had spread out in front of him.

Daddy could fix anything as long as it was

mechanical. Big machines, little machines. It didn't make any difference. My father could fix all of them.

His pipe was clinched tight in his teeth and the sticky sweet smell of his burning tobacco filled the tiny shed.

"There's a pair of fellows in suits here to see you," I said, a little breathless from the run across the yard. "I don't think they want you to fix anything. I think they just want to talk."

Daddy smiled and stood up from the worktable. "Then I guess we better go in the house and see what's going on."

My father was a tall man, skinny as a rail as the saying went. He had black hair slicked back with Brylcreem. Some folks said he looked Italian, but that was mainly because he'd spent so much time out in the sun that his skin was all brown and leathery looking. He always wore a blue work shirt with the sleeves rolled up past his elbows even in the summer.

Daddy had been a drilling supervisor at Murphy Oil and a real good one from what everybody said, but one day back in '39 something happened out on one of the rigs and Daddy came home, put his lunch pail on the high shelf up in the pantry and announced that he'd never work for Murphy or any oil company again. And that was that.

My father didn't do much but hang around the house for a few weeks. He'd sit at the kitchen table and take old radios apart and put them back together. Finally other folks started bringing him their busted radios and percolators and mix masters and stuff to fix and Daddy cleared out a space in the old shed out near the chicken coop and went into the small appliance repair business.

Daddy never hurried anywhere. Even after I told him about the two visitors, he ambled across the yard as if he were just heading up to the house for a drink of water.

Back in the living room, Mama had served ice tea to the two men, who were sitting on the blue sofa when Daddy and I came in. They stood up and shook hands all around. Mama brought Daddy a glass of tea. He drained half of it in one gulp.

"It's good to see you again, Mr. Ches," Taggert said.

Daddy nodded. "What can I do for you?" He sounded unfriendly and I could tell my father didn't have much truck with the Taggert fellow.

The first plunks of the summer rain hit the roof. The smell of Daddy's tobacco overpowered the living room.

Taggert and Quinn sat back down, balancing their hats in their laps. Mama leaned on the doorsill, wiping flour off her hands with her apron.

"Mr. Ches," Taggert said. "We need to talk some business if you have a few minutes."

Daddy shrugged.

Taggert turned and looked at me. "Son, why don't you run outside and play for a while. This won't take long."

"It's raining," I said, indicated the front window where the summer storm was pelting the glass.

Taggert gnawed on his lower lip.

"Come on, Ricky." Mama came to Taggert's rescue. "Let's you and me run out to the henhouse and fix up those stalls like we been promising to do since school let out."

I didn't want to leave the living room. Something was going on. Something big. You could just feel it in the air. You could see it on Daddy's face, hear it in Mama's voice. This was important. And I had to go out and fix up the stalls in the henhouse. I was not happy.

But I went.

By the time Mama and I hammered all the loose boards back into the chicken stalls, replaced the straw, swept out the walkway, and went back to the house, Taggert and Quinn were gone.

Daddy sat in the chair in the living room, staring out the window at the rain. The drops pounded the glass and ran down the panes in fast flowing rivulets.

It was getting dark, but Daddy hadn't turned on any lights. He just sat there in the chair, smoking his pipe and staring out the window. He didn't even turn around when Mama and I came back into the house. He just sat and stared and smoked. I'd never seen him look like that.

"Daddy? Are you all right?" I stood in the doorway to the kitchen, fighting back that awful sense that something was bad wrong.

My father didn't say anything. Blue smoke drifted out of his pipe and floated toward the ceiling. The room got darker and darker.

Two weeks later, he and Mama and I took a train

down to New Orleans, got on a big ship, and headed for Venezuela.

⟪ 2 ⟫

That summer of 1941, war clouds hung over the world. The German army had just charged into the Soviet Union, and the last thing on earth I wanted to do was leave El Dorado and travel halfway around the world to Venezuela. But life is so weird. That summer I was almost thirteen, a teenager. One minute I was safe and sound in the only house I'd ever lived in, reading comics, playing baseball with my friends, fishing, and riding my bike, and the next minute I was on a ship heading to a place I'd never even heard of before.

It reminded me of the time, a couple of years earlier, when Elmer Baylen and his family suddenly moved to California. Elmer and I were good friends. I used to walk over to his house, which was just down the road from our house, and eat oatmeal raisin cookies after school. Elmer and I would play catch out back in the pasture and take turns batting. Elmer was the one who taught me how to hit a baseball.

I even saw his older sister naked one time. The Baylens had an indoor toilet with a shower, and one day Elmer and I were walking down the hallway on our way out to the back to play ball and Elmer, just out of meanness, threw open the bathroom door and there was Ruby, who must have been about fifteen, standing there buck naked. She grabbed a towel, covered up, and yelled a cussword at Elmer. Elmer just laughed and laughed, and he and I ran out of the house and headed for the pasture.

I couldn't hit the ball a lick the rest of the afternoon.

Then that fall, Mr. Baylen, who hadn't had work in a couple of years, had to sell the house and head out to California to find a job. The Baylens packed up everything they owned in an old Ford, strapped battered suitcases on the roof and piled boxes in the back, and just drove away one day. I never heard from Elmer again.

But what was so bad was that me and the other fellows from school kept playing ball and doing our arithmetic and eating raisin cookies. But Elmer just wasn't there anymore.

And all of a sudden, right there in the summer of '41, it was me that wasn't there anymore.

And that really hurt.

In fairness, there had been lots of tension in the air that summer. President Roosevelt nationalized the army in the Philippines and put General MacArthur in charge of the troops. Daddy said that was a sure sign war was coming.

Daddy and Mama listened to the reporters like Gabriel Heatter and Walter Winchell every evening on the radio. Seemed like all those fellows ever talked about was all the bombing and killing over in Europe and Asia.

They never mentioned Venezuela.

I was gonna miss baseball more than anything. Even in seventh grade I was the starting catcher on our school baseball team. Only seventh grader on the whole team. I was big for my age, a big ole freckled-face, redheaded country boy, who could hit the ball a mile. Only all of a sudden I wasn't on the team anymore. Somebody else would be catching for the Oilers.

I don't remember much about the two weeks before we left. I know I threw a tantrum just about every day, and I remember I took my Louisville Slugger outside one evening and beat up the chicken coop pretty bad.

Mama and Daddy just let my tantrums go. I guess they figured I had to get all that hurt and anger out of my system. One day I ran out of the house and kept running across the pasture out back. While I was running, I started crying and I kept running and crying until I got all the way over to Bodcau Creek where I collapsed on the bank and threw up until there was nothing left in my belly.

I didn't cry anymore after that. But that didn't mean I wasn't still hurting inside. You don't have to be crying to be hurting.

One thing that really made me mad was that Daddy wouldn't even tell me why we were moving to South America. He said he'd tell me in good time. Mama tried to make me feel better by showing me a map and pointing out Venezuela, which sat right above the equator, surrounded by Colombia, Brazil, and British

Guiana. The northern border was the Caribbean.

Even when I knew where we were going, the knowledge didn't make me feel any better. Venezuela might as well have been surrounded by Mars and Venus and Pluto for all I cared. All I knew was Venezuela was one heck of a long way from El Dorado, Arkansas.

Daddy went down to the public library and checked out every book they had on Venezuela. Both of them. He spent every evening after supper curled up in his chair in the living room, reading those books as if his life depended on it.

Mama took to drinking whiskey.

She'd never been much of a drinking woman, but after Daddy announced we were all moving to South America, Mama started having a little nip of bourbon every now and then while she listened to records on the phonograph. She played Glenn Miller's "Chattanooga Choo Choo" until the record got all scratchy, and sometimes she'd stare off into nowhere, her face a mask of sadness.

Mama had reddish hair like mine and a thickish body and a doughy face. But she also had emerald green eyes that could sparkle when she talked about Glenn Miller or bridge, which was this card game she was crazy about.

Actually Mama's drinking did me a good turn just a couple of days before we left El Dorado. That afternoon, she was a bit in her cups, and she found me out behind the chicken coop, throwing a tennis ball against the sidewall and then fielding grounders.

Mama lurched around the corner and pulled up

short when she saw me.

"I know all this is hard on you." She slurred her words.

"Yes, ma'am," I said, throwing the ball back against the wall.

Mama folded her arms across her chest and leaned against the henhouse to keep from swaying. "Well, I imagine you've been around long enough to know life's often full of suffering."

I nodded.

"Least that's what the Good Book teaches."

I nodded again.

"And we do what we can to get through."

"Yes, ma'am."

"So here's a little something for you." She reached into the pocket of her apron and pulled out a crumpled dollar bill. "I thought you might like to take this and go down to Jack's and get yourself some of them comic books you like. Something to keep you busy on the trip."

I took the money. "You mean I can spend the whole dollar?"

A faint smile crossed her face.

I stuffed the money in my jeans pocket. "Thanks, Mama."

Mama's eyes teared up and she spun around and lurched back to the house.

A dollar was a heck of a lot of money. I mean a loaf of store-bought bread didn't cost but eight cents, and if you had a whole dollar, you were a rich man. Or a rich boy in my case.

I hopped on my bike before Mama changed her mind. The ride to town took about twenty minutes, and I peddled right up to the front of Jack's Newsstand.

Jack's was my favorite place in El Dorado. The front door faced the train depot, and inside Jack's was always cool, no matter how hot the summer day. Winter or summer a big ceiling fan stirred the wonderful musty, bookie, smoky smell of the place.

The left side of the store had wooden racks filled with newspapers and magazines—*The Dallas Morning News, Shreveport Times, The New Orleans Picayune, Arkansas Gazette, Life, Look, Colliers, The Saturday Evening Post.* In the center of the room was a pair of wire racks that spun around and held paperback books, with pictures of half-naked ladies and gun-wielding detectives on the covers.

The racks sat right in front of a door that led to the back room of Jack's Newsstand. I'd never been back there, but I knew that beyond that door the men of El Dorado gathered for legendary poker games. Growing up in El Dorado, you knew you'd reached manhood when they let you play in the poker games in back of the newsstand.

I guess, since we were leaving for South America, I'd never get in one of the games. It was just as well. I didn't know how to play poker anyway.

The Mutual Game of the Day was playing on a radio in the back of the store. The New York Giants were playing the St. Louis Cardinals.

Mr. Jack himself sat on a high stool behind the glass counter, reading a paper and smoking a cigarette.

No matter when you went to Jack's Newsstand, there was Jack, reading his paper and smoking. He had silver hair that always looked like it needed combing and a sandpaper beard. Jack didn't look up when I came in.

"Cards are whippin' the Giants. Lon Warneke's pitching a shutout into the 7th," he growled, snapping his newspaper. Lon Warneke was from Arkansas and everybody rooted for him whenever he pitched.

"I reckon the Redbirds got a chance at the series this year," I said. "They got good hittin' and good pitchin'."

"That's what you say every year." Jack still didn't look up from his paper.

"Yes, sir. But this is the year. I just know it."

"Never hurts to hope." Jack snapped his paper again.

"No, sir. I reckon not." Having covered the topic of baseball, I wandered into the rear of the store and Jack went back to the news.

In the back of the store there was another wooden rack, only this one was chock-full of comic books. Hundreds of them. All my favorites—*Batman, Captain Marvel, Wonder Woman, Captain America, Superman* and my favorite, the *Blue Beetle*.

I loved every one of them. I loved the drawings with all the colors and shadows, and I loved the wonderful characters that were not real but somehow more than real. I loved the stories—the bad guys would almost win, but the heroes would somehow save the day in the end. That's what heroes did.

Never in my life had I bought more than one comic

at a time, and the thought of buying ten made my head swim. I kept fingering the dollar in my pocket just to make sure the money was still there. I finally picked out ten comics and just holding that many in my hands made my heart pound like a jackhammer.

I put the comics and my dollar bill on the counter in front of Mr. Jack.

"The Germans are giving the Russians hell," he said, keeping his eyes on his paper. "Them panzers are cutting down the Bolshies like a scythe going through winter wheat. Cutting down all them young fellows. Lord, what's the world coming to?" Jack shook his grizzled head.

"My daddy says 'fore too long, we're gonna step in and stop the Germans," I said.

"If we do, I hope it's long before your time to be a soldier, partner." Sometimes Jack talked like the old cowboys in the two reelers.

"Well, if the war goes on, I reckon I'd do my duty." I hadn't really given it much thought, but it sounded like what a patriotic American boy ought to say.

Mr. Jack looked up from his paper and nailed me with a cold stare. "What's going on, son?"

I thought he meant all the comics I was getting. But he was talking about something else.

"Something mysterious is going on all over town. I never seen the likes of it."

"Mysterious?"

"You bet," Jack said. "Ed Taggert and a couple of the best Murphy field men just up and quit the company. Moved away is what I hear. Nobody knows where to. They just up and quit good jobs. Times being what they are, that sounds mighty strange to me."

"Yes, sir. It does."

"And I'm hearing rumors about secret government agents right here in town. That's mysterious for sure. And this morning I hear you and your folks are leaving us."

"Yes, sir. We are. We're going all the way to South America."

"South America. Well, if that don't beat all." Mr. Jack let out a long sigh. "The Oilers are gonna sure miss you behind the plate next year. Folks say you're the best catcher they've had over at the school in years." He counted my comic books. "South America. Lord, that's a long way to go," he mumbled.

"Sure is."

"Well, pardner, you're gonna need a lot of these here comic books to keep you company seeing as how you're going that far. I reckon you ought to pick yourself out a couple more. This here dollar will cover it."

I went back to the racks and added *The Three Musketeers* Classic Comic and the new *Captain Marvel* to my collection.

Secret agents? Mr. Jack was right. Something big was going on, and I had a feeling my daddy was right smack in the middle of it all.

"Thanks, Mr. Jack," I said, pausing at the door, looking around the newsstand for what I suspected would be the last time.

"You ever get back this way, you come see me, you hear." Jack's head was back in his newspaper, but his voice had a quake in it.

"I sure will," I said. "I promise." I walked out of the newsstand and choked back a lump in my throat as I hopped on my bike.

≪ 3 ≫

The next thing I knew my parents and I were on a big gray freighter out of New Orleans called the *King of the Sea*, which had cabins for twenty or thirty passengers. I got seasick the first day out. And the second day.

By the third day, I was feeling better and got lost in the adventures of Batman and Robin and Captain Marvel. Then, late that afternoon, Daddy and I drifted up to the top deck and stood at the railing, just watching the white-capped sea roll by. The salty air smelled good and the day had been bright and sunny. Daddy and I just stood there for a long time and took it all in.

Then we had the first man-to-man talk we had ever had.

Both of us leaned on the railing, and, not looking at each other, talked out to the sea. Man-to-man talks are easier that way.

"I know all this has been hard on you," my father said.

"Yes, sir." I tried to keep the anger out of my voice.

"Well, I need to tell you what's going on. That might make some of this go down a little better."

"It might."

"You know I love you and your Mama more than anything else in the world."

I had never heard my father say anything remotely close to that sudden declaration of love. It took me off guard. I watched a couple of gulls that were circling the *King of the Sea*.

"But these are treacherous times and sometimes a man has other loyalties. Not instead of his family. But along with his family. You understand?"

I shrugged.

"I couldn't tell you the whole story before we left because Mr. Quinn asked me not to tell anyone. Not even you. I didn't want any of the fellows at your school to know exactly where we were going."

"Aren't we going to Venezuela like you said?" It came out with an edge. Maybe I should have just let out all my rage but I decided to keep it inside no matter what. That's what Captain Marvel would have done.

"Well, yes we are. But specifically we're going to an American oil camp on Lake Maracaibo. It's run by an outfit called Creole Oil. Creole is really Standard of New Jersey, but they use a different name in Venezuela. I'm going to be a drilling supervisor for the wells in the lake." Daddy paused and cleared his throat.

"I know you know about what's happening in Europe and this is . . . this is connected with all of that."

I turned and looked at Daddy. He had his pipe clinched between his teeth and sounded so serious it scared me a little.

"You told me and Mama you were never going to

work for an oil company again."

"And I meant it when I said it."

"Something bad happened out in the field back in Arkansas, didn't it? Something that made you quit Murphy Oil."

"That's it in a nutshell," my father said. "Ed Taggert was my boss and he refused to put in some safety equipment to protect the men working the wells. He said the company couldn't afford it. I wouldn't be a part of that. I love the oil business but not enough to put my men in harm's way."

"And now you're going back to work for Mr. Taggert?"

My father shook his head. "I've known Ed Taggert all my life. He's always been a stubborn old cuss, but he's very respected in the oil business."

"I don't understand," I said. "So you're moving me and Mama all the way to Venezuela to work for a man you wouldn't work for back in Arkansas. I don't get that."

"I know that sounds crazy," Daddy said. "Ed Taggert's an ornery old devil, but there's no man alive who knows more about drilling for oil than Ed. I guess when I think about it, Ed's no different than the rest of us. He's not all bad, but he's not all good either. I remember one time, Bobby Greene, one of our best workers on the rigs, had a little girl and she got terrible sick. Doctor bills were higher than an Ozark mountain. Ed Taggert covered all of 'em. Bobby never knew who paid those bills. But his little girl got all right."

"Mr. Taggert did that?"

"He sure did. Only a couple of us knew about it. Don't you go telling anybody, you hear?"

I made the zipper sign over my lips.

"Ed's a good family man. Got two grown sons who live up in Little Rock. Good men both of them. And Ed's devoted to Martha. They been married thirty years."

"Mr. Taggert sounds okay. Except for . . ."

"Right. But I reckon that's true of most of us. Ed's honest and knows what he's doing on the oil rigs. And our country is gonna need a lot of oil in the next year or so. I reckon my country's worth going back on what I said earlier about never working for an oil company again."

"The war in Europe?"

"Yep. America can't stay out of the war much longer," my father said. "We can't sit by and watch this Hitler fellow take over the world. He's mean at heart and pretty soon Uncle Sam's going to have to step in and teach him a lesson. And you know what this country is going to need to beat him and his Nazi thugs?"

I looked back at the gulls and shrugged. "Oil?"

"That's right, son. Oil. We need oil right now. President Roosevelt has pledged planes, ships, and jeeps and such to the British and the Russians and they're going need oil to run those machines. And we aim to give it to 'em."

I watched the whitecaps roll over the blue-green ocean.

"President Roosevelt himself has charged Ed with

putting together an . . . well . . . an all-star team of an oil crew to get the wells at Lake Maracaibo up and going full force."

The gulls swooped low, near the bow of the freighter.

"The fellows heading down to Venezuela are the best men in the American oil fields," my father said. "And Ed promised to put in all the safety equipment I asked for."

I chewed on that for a while. Part of me was so proud of Daddy I could have busted my buttons. An all-star. Like Ted Williams and Marty Marion. But part of me still felt a sadness so powerful it almost doubled me over. El Dorado was long gone.

"Who is Mr. Quinn?" I asked after a while. "The fellow that came to the house with Mr. Taggert."

Daddy took his pipe out of his mouth and packed the tobacco tight in the bowl. "Government man," he said in a low voice. "Works directly for the president."

Mr. Jack had been right. A secret agent. Right there in El Dorado.

"But the camp will be nice for you and your Mama," Daddy said, resting his elbows on the railing. "Taggert says they have a nice club and a swimming pool and a school, and they'll be other kids your age."

"Do they play baseball?"

"Sure. I reckon anyplace you find American kids you'll find baseball."

I puffed up my cheeks and blew out the air. I pretended I was a soldier who was shipping off for duty in Venezuela. Private Parker on a dangerous and important assignment. Just like the heroes in the comics. The thought made me feel better.

At least for a while.

We docked in Maracaibo and Mr. Taggert met us as soon as we stepped off the ship and hustled us off to a waiting car. He said someone from the company would look after our bags and trunks and get them to the camp. He had a dented up old Ford, and we drove straight to a ferry dock on the other side of the city.

The trip across the town took my breath away. I had never seen anything like Maracaibo. El Dorado was a sleepy little hamlet in south Arkansas. Maracaibo was a whole different ball game. The place was so . . . alive. Narrow streets crammed full of dirty cars, horse carts, and donkeys with their backs piled high with stuff.

We drove past a market with little wooden stalls, where men in droopy mustaches sold fruit and vegetables. Whole skinned rabbits hung from poles, blood dripping down in puddles. Dark-skinned women, their heads covered with blankets, ducked in and out of the stalls, pointing and talking in loud voices.

The car crawled past a crowded street corner where a handful of boys just a couple of years older than me gathered around a storefront, smoking cigarettes. They were a tough bunch. One of them wore an Indian headband and had the beginning of a mustache. A tall muscular boy had cut the sleeves out of his shirt to show off his pumped-up arms. He wore a knife in a scabbard on his belt.

Our car slowed and the boys peered in at me. Their mouths turned up in visible sneers. I felt relieved when the car speeded up and we left them behind.

Mr. Taggert drove the car right onto the boat at the ferry dock, and a pair of rough-looking men with no shirts on lashed the Ford down with practiced efficiency.

The ferry ride across the lake took about an hour. Back home in Arkansas, lakes were places you went to fish and picnic and maybe paddle around in a canoe. Most of the time you could see the trees on the other side. But Lake Maracaibo was more like the ocean. The deep blue-green water quivered with whitecaps that lashed at the side of the ferry and the lake was so big I couldn't see across to the other side.

Way off to the south I could barely make out the outline of some of the offshore oil rigs, which rose out of the water like an army of giant insects.

I was too nervous to sit still and hopped back and forth from one side of the ferry to the other, trying to see everything. The humidity rivaled Arkansas on a July day, and my shirt was soaked with sweat by the time we landed at the camp.

We got back into the Ford and drove off the ferry.

Driving into the Creole Camp on the shores of Lake Maracaibo was like driving back into history, straight into a cowboy town that belonged in a Tom Mix western movie. The streets were narrow, unpaved, dusty, and full of deep holes. There were no other cars on the street.

"This is the main street," Mr. Taggert said,

swerving to avoid a small crater. "Over yonder is the administration office, and right there on your right, Dixie, is the company store."

My mother's skin had turned the color of paste.

"Right down there to my left"—Taggert spit a big wad of tobacco out the window— "is the British and Dutch compounds. They're all good folks once you get to know them. And just past those houses is the German compound. There ain't many of them left. Just a handful of engineers and geologist who have worked for the company since they started operations here back in '21. The Germans pretty much keep to themselves. You never see them at the Club or anywhere. They just do their job and go back to their compound. Suits me just fine."

Mama's eyes were wide ovals of shock, as she took in the truth of her new home. Her lower lip quavered.

A pair of men in Stetson hats, blue jeans, and rough work shirts came out of the company store. They looked over at the Ford and gave a little salute. Mr. Taggert saluted back. The men proceeded to the hitching rail at the side of the store, where they untied and mounted a pair of chestnut horses.

"Way on down this road, as far north as you can go, is the native camp," Mr. Taggert said. "Ricky, son, listen to me carefully on this."

I tore my eyes away from the men on the horses.

"The natives don't never come up here. They have their own store and everything they need right in their camp. But you don't ever go over to their compound. You hear me, son? They're a worthless, shiftless lot and

I reckon some of them would cut your throat for a quarter."

I was in the backseat with Mama and I couldn't see Daddy's face up in the front seat with Mr. Taggert, but there was something about the way my father didn't say anything that made me feel even more nervous.

The car bounced and lurched on down the unpaved street.

"Ah, now there's the Club." Mr. Taggert indicated a low yellowish stucco building with a flat roof and a wide shaded veranda across the front. A man in a white hat sat in a wicker chair on the porch. He waved to Mr. Taggert. Mr. Taggert waved back. There were tables shaded by big umbrellas on the roof. "The Club's where our folks go when they want to unwind. They have a bar and card tables and ping-pong for the young'uns. It's a right nice place if I do say so myself. You like ice cream, Ricky?"

"Sure."

"Then you're gonna love the Club. They keep chocolate and strawberry as well as vanilla stocked all the time. They always have peach on the 4th of July."

"Great."

"I thought you'd like that. When my boys were growing up, they couldn't get enough ice cream." Mr. Taggert let out a little laugh.

My father still didn't say a word.

"On the other side of the Club are the bachelor barracks. Nothing but American boys and every one of 'em a good worker. They'll get the job done for you, Mr. Ches. I guarantee it."

My father managed a slight nod.

Past the Club, we started down a street lined with small clapboard houses. The grass in the front yards was yellowed and trampled down to the dirt. The houses sat on brick stilts and had screen porches in the front. Most of the screens had gaping rips in them and a lot of the houses begged for paint. There were some scrubby-looking trees and a couple of tire swings that sat lonely and idle. A little red wagon with a broken wheel sat on someone's front walkway. There wasn't a soul anywhere.

Taggert grew silent as we drove deeper into the neighborhood.

Mama absentmindedly shredded a Kleenex in her lap.

We took a right and then a left and Mr. Taggert came to a stop in front of a single story house in the middle of the block. The house had been battered by the weather and its original green paint had turned a grayish color. The yard was a patch of dirt. The place reminded me of the sharecropper's shacks back in Arkansas.

"Here we are," Mr. Taggert said with false cheeriness. "Number 56. This is the one the company assigned you folks. I think you'll like it. A real homey place. Your bags will be along real soon. Why don't you all just go right on in and make yourself at home. Then first thing in the morning, Mr. Ches, why don't you come on up to the administration building, and we can get started on getting these rigs producing what they ought to." He handed Daddy a key.

Mama and I piled out of the backseat and stood beside Daddy in the front yard. The green paint on the house had been applied carelessly, too thick in places where it sat in unsightly lumps. Mama let out a long mournful sigh. Daddy put his arm around her shoulder and pulled her close to him. I could see by the way Daddy looked at Mama that he loved her a whole bunch, but maybe not as much as working on the oil rigs. It was hard to tell.

"Oh, I almost forgot," Mr. Taggert called out from the car. "There's a right nice surprise waiting for you in the house. I know you're gonna like it. Bye now." He laughed out loud and drove off in a cloud of brownish dust.

« 4 »

"What's been keeping you, you worthless old toad?"

Daddy stopped just inside the door. There was no mistaking the booming voice. It belonged to Uncle Harry.

Mama and I crowded in behind Daddy. The living room was tiny and all the furniture was covered in white sheets except for a worn wooden rocking chair that held Uncle Harry's massive frame.

Uncle Harry's beaming smile would light up the darkest night. His head was completely shaved, tanned leather brown from the sun. He was a muscular man and even sitting down he radiated raw strength and power. At the moment he was drinking a bottle of Lone Star beer. Three empties sat beside his chair.

Uncle Harry wasn't really my uncle. We just called him that. He was my Daddy's best friend in the whole world. Rumor had it Uncle Harry could perform magic on busted oil rigs and he and my father had been friends since the wildcat days of the east Texas oil fields. We hadn't seen him in a year or so. Daddy said Uncle Harry had gone back to working the rigs in Texas where the two of them started out.

"Welcome to Paradise," Uncle Harry said, saluting with the beer bottle. "Company made me the welcoming committee. Figured it would go down better that way. The Creole Camp is not so bad once you get used to it. But you could probably say the same thing about hell."

"It's good to see you, Harry," Daddy said. "And that's no lie."

Uncle Harry bounced out of the chair and grabbed Daddy in a big bear hug. Daddy just laughed. Then Uncle Harry let go of Daddy and turned to Mama who hung back in the doorframe. "Ah, in a place sorely lacking in beauty, you are a sight for sore eyes, Dixie."

Mama blushed then put out her arms and she and Uncle Harry hugged.

"And who is this?" Uncle Harry turned to me. "Must be one of the new roustabouts. A lad who could do a full day's work and then dance the young belles off their feet every night."

I laughed. "It's me, Uncle Harry. Ricky."

"My god, you've grown a foot since I saw you last. How are you lad?"

"Okay. I guess."

"Well, come in, come in. We've got some catching up to do. There's more beer in the icebox."

Mama headed straight for the kitchen.

Along with the beer, Uncle Harry had brought a bottle of Coca-Cola for me and the four of us had an impromptu welcoming party. We pulled the sheets off of the furniture, except for this one mysterious piece in the corner of the living room that Uncle Harry said was his housewarming present.

We opened all the windows, but the breeze that blew between the rooms felt like a blast from a hot stove. There were large water stains on the ceiling that looked like brown clouds and the floors were scuffed and scarred.

Daddy dug up a small oscillating fan in a storage closet, and we settled into the living room in front of the fan. Daddy and Mama sat on the ragged sofa, Uncle Harry back in his chair, and I sat on the floor, sipping my Coke, making the cool sweetness last as long as possible.

"So what's the setup, Harry?" Daddy's blue shirt was dark with sweat.

"Well, I've only been here a week," Uncle Harry said. "And to be honest with you, about all I've done is lose my stake at the poker table over in the bachelor barracks. Matter of fact, I was hoping you might spot me a little until payday."

Mama smiled and shook her head.

"Glad to know some things never change. Harry, I swear you are the worst poker player on God's earth."

"I'll drink to that." Harry raised his beer bottle and laughed his big booming laugh.

"You'll drink to anything," Daddy said.

Everyone laughed.

Uncle Harry had that effect on people. No matter what folks were worrying about or how blue they felt, Harry always seemed to get a laugh and a smile out of them.

"Tell me about the rigs," Daddy said with a touch

of seriousness.

"The offshore derricks have been neglected for a while."

Daddy nodded. "Then we'll have our work cut out for us."

Mama finished her beer and went to the kitchen.

Uncle Harry looked down at me like he wasn't sure he should say what he wanted to say with me in the room. He must have decided it was okay. "You think the winds of war are blowing our way, Ches?"

"Sooner than anyone thinks." Daddy took a thoughtful sip of beer. "I don't care what that group of antiwar naysayers the American Firsters have to say, we can't let that madman Hitler rule the world."

"I'll drink to that." Uncle Harry raised his bottle. Nobody laughed this time.

Mama returned to the living room with a fresh bottle of Lone Star.

Daddy and Uncle Harry talked some more about the company, the rigs, and some of the men they knew who were coming to work in the camp. They really did sound like an all-star team. Finally, Uncle Harry said he wanted to give us our last welcoming present and be on his way. He smiled like a magician about to reveal a new trick, stood up, and with great fanfare pulled the white sheet off the mysterious piece of furniture.

It was an upright phonograph. Old, battered, and scratched but still a phonograph. "I dug this beauty up in a closet over at the Club," Uncle Harry said. "Polished her up and took her apart and gave her a good repair and cleaning. I dare say she plays better now than the day she was born. I was gambling you wouldn't be leaving home without those records you love, Dixie. Am I right?"

Mama's mouth dropped open. She stared at the phonograph for a minute and then started crying. "Oh, Harry," she managed to say with tears streaming down her cheeks. "Only you can make a hell like this seem a little bit like heaven."

I stole a glance at my father. He started to say something, shrugged his shoulders, and jammed his pipe in his mouth. He chewed on the pipe stem like a starving dog with a bone. He never took his eyes off Mama.

* * *

The next couple of weeks were long and lonely. Every morning, Daddy and Mama got up before dawn and Mama packed Daddy's lunch pail, and he was gone to work on the offshore rigs with Uncle Harry, walking the half mile or so from our little house to the dock. He rarely came home before dark.

Mama spent a couple of days scrubbing out the house and trying to make the place as close to home as possible. Our bags and trunks arrived and Mama listened to the Andrews Sisters and Glenn Miller on her new phonograph while she hung curtains and dusted and polished and sipped bourbon from her ever-present tumbler.

She ventured out of the house after a few days and discovered a regular afternoon bridge game at the Club and life started to feel something like normal.

I hung around the house, and read and reread my comics, went out in the backyard, tossed my tennis ball against the side of the house, and fielded grounders. Mama made oatmeal cookies, and I read more comics and gobbled down the cookies at the kitchen table.

I missed my friends from El Dorado Junior High and fishing Bodcau Creek and Jack's Newsstand. My only friends in the Creole Camp were Clark and Lois and Jimmy and Billy Batson. Only when I said "Shazam!" nothing changed. It was probably just as well, since there were no bad guys to battle anyway.

I should have been more patient.

The camp school wasn't supposed to start for almost a month, and boredom finally pushed me out of the house. The men who lived in the camp all went to work on the rigs at dawn, and the women either did housework or went to the Club, so the camp felt like a ghost town.

At first I just put on a pair of khaki pants and an old white T-shirt and my beat up U.S. Keds and just wandered around. I walked all the way to the end of the housing section and discovered a wide field that ended with what looked like the jungle in a Tarzan movie. I listened for a minute, expecting to hear Johnny Weissmuller give his *Lord of the Jungle* call, but the jungle stayed quiet.

At the other end of the housing section, just across the way from the bachelor barracks, I found the school. It wasn't much. A one-story stone building. I tried looking in the windows but they were covered in dust.

Judging from the size of the school, there couldn't have been more than five or six rooms. Back behind the school, I found a baseball field, and for a moment, I felt really happy because a baseball field meant there was baseball.

But the field wasn't exactly Yankee Stadium. It was just a sandy, rocky expanse with a dilapidated wooden backstop. But the field did have real bases and a row of wooden bleachers that looked like if you sat on them, you'd be pulling splinters out of your butt for a week. I sat in the bleachers anyway.

The day was hot and windless. All my happiness at finding the field slowly evaporated and I felt like crying. I missed the evening baseball games back in El Dorado. I even missed El Dorado Junior High and ole Miss Jameson who popped me on the knuckles with a yardstick when she caught me chewing gum in English class. I missed looking forward to the high school football games in the crisp fall weather in Arkansas.

I hated the Creole Camp and I didn't care what was happening in Russia or England or France or how much oil they needed. I just wanted to go home.

I finally abandoned the bleachers and wandered away from the baseball field, past an open pasture, which was covered in brown patchy grass and would have been a pretty good place to play football. The jungle picked up on the far side of the field and I turned back toward this dirt road that ended where the jungle began. A little way down the road, I found a bunch of huge discarded concrete pipes. I could stand upright in them and jump as high as I could and still not touch the top. I wandered around in the pipes for a while yelling "hello" and listening to the echoes.

Lost in my wandering and "helloing" in the pipes, I quit paying attention to what I was doing, and when I got to the exit of the pipe, I looked up and realized that I was face-to-face with a dragon.

I pulled up short, too frightened to move. The dragon came up to my waist and was silhouetted by the light at the pipe opening. He had a scaly body and his blood red tongue flicked in and out of his mouth. He turned his head and looked right at me like he had just stumbled on a tasty lunch.

I held my breath. Sweat broke out on my forehead. I fought the urge to turn and run as fast as I could back the other way through the pipe, but I knew if I did the dragon would catch me in a flash.

As my eyes adjusted to the dark, I realized the dragon was actually a giant, and I mean a *giant*, lizard. The thing was bigger than Billy Tom's hound dog back home. A whole lot bigger.

I looked around the pipe for some kind of a weapon, but the pickings were slim. I did find a rock. Not a very big one, but big enough to coldcock the sucker between the eyes if he charged me.

Me and the monster lizard just stood there for a while, looking each other over. I was sweating and I was sure the thing could hear my heart pounding in my chest. I held the rock with two fingers like you hold a baseball. We stared each other down.

Then, suddenly, the lizard turned around and scurried out of the pipe, disappearing across the road and into the jungle. I guess I wasn't such a tasty lunch after all.

I whirled around and sprinted to the far end of the pipe. Before I ran through the opening, I stopped and looked both ways. No lizards or dragons. I hit the road at a full gallop and didn't slow down until I jumped up on the front porch back at our house, bolted through the door, slammed it behind me, and leaned my back on the thin wood, panting and gasping for air.

That was the most exciting thing that happened to me the first couple of weeks at the Creole Oil Camp.

Until I met Hannah. And everything changed.

《 5 》

For lack of anything else to do, I took to going over to the baseball field every day. Just in case. I'd take my mitt and my Louisville Slugger and sit in the little bleachers, hoping somebody might show up. I even took along a couple of comics and sat in the shade of the stands and read *Captain Marvel* and the *Blue Beetle* cover to cover to pass the time. But no one came.

I started packing peanut butter and jelly sandwiches and homemade oatmeal raisin cookies in a brown paper sack and hiking over to the field and waiting in the stands. Still nobody came.

Until late one Saturday afternoon.

I rounded the corner of the stone school building, my bat over my shoulder and my mitt tucked under my arm and there they were. Boys playing baseball on the field. I stopped and rubbed my eyes and looked again. The boys were still there.

They weren't really playing. Four of them had a pepper game going in front of the bleachers and a couple of them were playing catch out by second base. Way out in the outfield four dark-haired, dark-skinned boys about my age were playing four-cornered catch.

Two of them didn't have gloves. They all wore dirty canvas pants. None of them wore shirts.

"Hey!" one of the guys in the pepper game yelled as I approached the stands. "You must be the new drilling supervisor's kid. Man! I heard you weren't but twelve."

"That's me." I said.

"Geez, you're a big one." The boy had sandy hair and buckteeth.

"You wanna play? We should have a game going in a few minutes."

"Sure."

"We usually can scrape up enough fellows every Saturday for a real game." The boy shot me a toothy grin. "I'm Sonny Cole. That's my brother Will." He indicated a smaller boy with the same sandy coloring and a nose that was too big for his face. "Our daddy's a company geologist. We just got back from the states yesterday. Every three years you work down here the company gives you three-month paid vacation stateside. We're from Bastrop, Louisiana."

Three years? You had to stay in the camp three years before going home? In three years Billy Tom and all my buddies would be at El Dorado High. Three years. My heart sank.

"El Dorado, Arkansas," I said, pulling myself together.

"I been there. That's Murphy Oil, ain't it?"

"Yeah."

"Man, I'm glad you're here. It's hard to get enough fellows for a game. With me and Will and a couple of other fellows back in the States, we ain't had a game all summer. Even with you playing, we'll have to let the Venezuelans play. But I warn you though. Keep a watch on 'em. They all carry knives. They don't talk no English and nobody likes 'em being here, but I tell you, those four out in the outfield are good ball players. We have to split 'em up when we make the teams. Otherwise they'd win every time."

I watched the four Venezuelans playing catch. I didn't see where they could be carrying a knife. They were shirtless and wore canvass pants held up by ropes. "Fine with me. I just want to play some ball." I put down my bat and put on my mitt.

"A catcher. Great. We can really use you." Sonny backed up a few steps and tossed the baseball to me. The ball made a familiar thump in the pocket of my glove. I tossed the ball back, not too hard, but with enough zip to let Sonny know I was a player. He caught the ball and threw it back.

My eyes wandered past Sonny and I saw a man near the edge of the outfield. He had on a Stetson and wore a pistol in a black holster by his side. He also carried a shotgun in the crook of his arm.

"Who's that?" I said, indicating the man.

"Ah, somebody said the Indians are acting up. The company sends a guard over in case something happens."

"The Indians?"

"Yeah," Sonny said. "The Motilone Indians down in the southwest. They used to live around here, around the lake and all. Then the company came in and pushed 'em out. They're pretty mad about the whole thing. They used to fish the lake and used the asphalt that seeped up to patch their canoes. Every once in a while a raiding party of Motilones will attack some of our workers on the edge of the camp."

"No kidding?"

"Truth. But it's not as bad as it sounds. We've lived here three years. I've never seen the Motilones myself. But you never know." Sonny tossed the ball back to me. I caught it and rifled the baseball back to him. Even with the threat of an Indian attack and the possibility of being stuck in the Creole Camp for three years, the thumping of a baseball in my mitt was the best feeling in the world.

The sun bathed the field in sticky warmth and a slight breeze kissed us with gentle gusts. It was a perfect baseball afternoon.

Except for the man with the guns in the outfield.

"Maybe you could catch for both teams. I've got a mask over yonder in my bag. We got fourteen players. We'll probably pick up—oh, swell. Here they come."

Sonny was looking over by the school building where two guys and two girls were rounding the corner. The boys looked about my age. They wore funny-looking little shorts and pressed white shirts. One of the girls had her hair done in a long blonde braid that reached almost all the way down to her waist. The other girl looked like she might be a little older. She was skinny and had shiny wavy brown hair. She carried a baby on her hip.

"Here come the Germans," Sonny said, catching

my return throw with one hand. *"Sieg Heil!"* He spit on the third base line. "We're lucky there's not many of them. Can you believe this? We got to play with Venezuelans and Krauts. Geez. But man, if we don't let 'em play, we ain't got enough guys for a game."

The German kids approached the bleachers. They nodded politely at Sonny and me. Sonny didn't bother to look at them. The smallest boy had a baseball glove that looked like a relic from the 1920s. The fingers weren't even laced together. The other boy had a regular looking glove. Neither one of them had a ball.

I couldn't take my eyes off of them. Real Germans. Nazi boys and Nazi girls. I had never seen a real live one in my life. Real honest-to-goodness Germans.

The boys stood off to one side of the bleachers, but Sonny didn't offer to let them play catch with us.

The girls spread a blanket underneath the bleachers in the shade. They propped the chubby little baby up on the blanket and entertained the little boy with a tiny red rattle. They talked to the baby in a foreign language, which I guessed was German.

In a few minutes we divided up into two teams. Like most sandlot baseball games this one had its own way of doing things. Two of the Venezuelan players went right to home plate. The other two stood out by the pitcher's mound. The two German boys joined the Venezuelans at home. Then Sonny pointed at a couple of other guys who trotted out to the pitcher's mound. Automatically a couple of other ones headed for the team at home. The whole ritual just took a couple of minutes.

"You'll catch for both teams," Sonny said, tossing me a catcher's mask from his bag. "But you get to bat twice."

"Good deal."

"Romulo usually pitches for them. He's the tall kid with the scar. Get ready behind the plate, he can bring the heat."

The pitcher's mound team fanned out into the field. "We're the Yankees," their first baseman yelled. Y'all were the Yankees last time."

"We'll be the Cards," Sonny yelled back. "Marty and Stan and Enos. Yeah!"

The stars of the St. Louis Cardinals. Wow! These guys were talking my language. Being on the field was the next best thing to being back in El Dorado.

Romulo walked to the pitcher's mound and grinned when he saw my catcher's mitt. He signaled for a couple of warm up pitches. I nodded back and got in my crouch.

Bring the heat? The guy threw fire. Smack! The ball hit in the center of the mitt, and despite the padding, my palm burned. He was a lot faster than anybody back in El Dorado.

The first batter was Sonny's brother. He took a couple of good cuts, but missed Romulo's fastball by a mile. He popped the third pitch up to the third baseman.

Romulo struck out the next batter.

Sonny came up and knocked the dirt off his cleats. "I told you he could fire the ball," he said, stepping into the batter's box. "I don't know where a stupid native kid learned to pitch like that."

I thumped my mitt and let out a little chatter. "Swing batter, swing batter. Batter, batter, batter."

Romulo reared back and fired the pitch. The ball broke to the outside and Sonny swung at the air. I missed the ball and it rolled back to the backstop.

I retrieved the ball, called "time out," and trotted out to the mound where I handed the ball back to Romulo. "Hey, great curve, man. But I gotta know when that baby's coming."

Romulo had no idea what I was saying.

"Curve. You know, ball goes like this." I indicated a breaking ball.

Romulo nodded and smiled. "Si. Si." He was taller than I had thought at first. He had chiseled features and coppery skin. An ugly pink scar that ran from his hairline almost all the way to his jaw marred the left side of his face.

"We need a signal."

Romulo looked puzzled.

"Here. I laid my index finger across my chest. "One. This is a fastball. Fast. Ball. Like you were throwing." He studied my finger intensely. "Two." I held two fingers across my chest. "Curveball." I made the breaking ball motion with my hand.

Romulo's face lit up. "Si. Si." He nodded enthusiastically.

"Okay. Let's smoke 'em."

Romulo still looked puzzled. I could have said, "Let's all eat our underpants." The guy had no idea what I was saying. I shrugged and hoped for the best.

Trotting back to home plate, I noticed the German

girls had left the baby asleep on the blanket in the shade underneath the bleachers and had taken seats on the front row. The blonde with the long braid was chatting away. The brown-haired girl seemed to be watching the game. She was close enough to see the freckles across her nose. I smiled. She smiled back.

I got down in my crouch and gave the two-fingered signal between my legs. Romulo nodded just like in the big leagues. Then he broke a perfect curve off the outside of the plate. Sonny swung and missed. "Guy can pitch," Sonny said. "Don't call for no more curveballs," he growled between his teeth.

For some reason I didn't like that, so I gave the two-fingered signal again.

The next pitch broke to the inside. Sonny struck out.

"Whose side are you on?" Sonny sounded angry.

"Theirs," I said. "I'll be on yours in a minute."

"I gotta straighten you out, boy."

I just shrugged.

Sonny frowned at me. "Down here you can't ever forget whose side you're really on."

I didn't know what he was talking about. This was baseball. I was on the side of whatever team I was playing with.

And the game was fun. Sonny pitched for the Cards, and once he started throwing, he seemed to forget about striking out. I set up the same signals with him that I did with Romulo. Sonny wasn't a bad pitcher. Not in Romulo's league, but not bad.

The Yankees tagged him for a pair of doubles and

got a run in the second, but another one of the Venezuelan players on the Cards hammered a triple down the left field line and I drove him home with a dinky little single to right. I felt lucky to get my bat on Romulo's fastball.

After a while, the brutal heat, the pain of missing El Dorado, and everything else but baseball faded away. Romulo hit a double and one of the German boys hit a line shot single to left. Romulo sped around third and beat the throw from the outfield.

The Cards came back when Sonny hit a single and stole second on me. Then another guy drove him home. Tie game.

Romulo hit another double and the next batter struck out. The next one popped up and Sonny's brother made a nice catch at second. I was up with two outs.

The afternoon was fading toward evening, and the shadow of the school building pushed onto the infield. My shirt and pants were soaked with sweat, and I could feel gritty dirt spots on my face. The infielders were chattering up a storm.

I picked up my Louisville Slugger and swung the bat hard like DiMaggio or Williams. We needed a clutch hit. I stole another glance at the brown-haired German girl. She had her legs crossed and rested her elbow on her knee with her chin on her palm. She was really watching the game. The other girl fired nonstop chatter at the brown-haired girl like a tommy gun.

Then, just before I walked up to the plate, I glanced under the bleachers. And my heart stopped beating.

The baby was sitting up on the blanket, his chubby

little legs splayed out at an angle, his little hands pawing aimlessly at the air.

What made my heart stop and my blood turn to ice was the sight of a giant spider—tarantula—poised on the edge of the blanket. His hairy black legs were already up on the blue of the blanket and his fuzzy body was not far behind. He was heading straight for the baby.

We'd had tarantulas back in Arkansas. Some pretty big ones, in fact. But nothing like this monster. From where I was standing, the thing looked like it was as big as second base.

"Oh, geez." Just beyond the hairy spider on the blanket, I spotted three more tarantulas, moving in from the backside of the bleachers, fanning out to surround the baby.

I didn't know if tarantulas could hear, and I guess it didn't matter. I let out a war cry and sprinted for the bleachers, waving my baseball bat over my head like a club.

The brown-headed girl looked startled. The braided girl stopped in mid-sentence, followed my eyes, and let out a piercing scream when she saw the tarantulas.

I raced past the girls and charged underneath the bleachers. I hurdled the spiders on the outside and went after the one on the blanket. The one closest to the baby. Without thinking about what I was doing, I raised my baseball bat over my head and brought it down on the center of the tarantula's body. The blow made a squishy sound, but as I brought the bat back the thing popped up in the air.

The word in Arkansas was that tarantulas, if provoked, would jump several feet in the air and attack their prey. When the thing came off the ground, I stepped back and tried to line up my next blow. I glanced over my shoulder at the three spiders behind me. One of them scampered off to my right and then circled in toward me.

I took a quick step toward him, but he held his ground. The one I had slammed with the bat landed on his back, but rolled over and took a couple of steps toward me. I swung the bat as hard as I could and landed a solid blow, square in the middle of his back.

The baby started crying.

The other players and the two girls jumped up on the bleachers and looked down between the seats at me and the tarantulas on the sandy ground below. I located Sonny in the crowd of anxious faces. "Grab the other bat," I yelled. "Help me out."

Sonny's eyes bugged out of his head. He looked at the tarantulas and shook his head no.

The braided girl was screaming and sobbing and yelling stuff in German.

I hit the hairy spider again. Blood shot into the air. The baby cried louder.

I whirled on the other two spiders off to my left.

Suddenly one of them flipped up in the air. But he wasn't leaping at me. He just jumped a foot or so off the ground. I couldn't figure out what had happened until I spotted Romulo on the right side of the bleachers and realized what had happened. Romulo had hit the tarantula with a rock. He had a couple more stones in his hand and was circling under the bleachers to place himself between the baby and the remaining pair of spiders.

Knowing that Romulo had the baby covered, I charged. I swung the bat on a level line and made contact with the tarantula Romulo had hit with the rock. The blow from the Louisville Slugger sent the hairy critter flying out the back of the bleachers.

I brought the bat back just as the other spider attacked me, flying across the sandy ground on his hairy legs. Wham! The bat stopped his charge. Wham! Wham! I pounded the giant spider again and again. Spider blood flew everywhere. The thing bounced with each blow, the hairy legs twisting and turning.

Sweat poured into my eyes. I heard yelling echoing off the bottom of the bleachers and realized I was yelling at the top of my lungs.

Certain the tarantula was dead, I spun around. Romulo was chasing the last spider back toward the schoolhouse with a steady barrage of rocks. He was yelling at the thing in rapid-fire Spanish.

The brown-haired girl scrambled off the bleachers and ran past me. She scooped up the baby and started comforting him. He calmed down quicker than I did.

I was a mess. Panting, sweating, and shaking. Giant hairy spiders. Ugh!

"Thank you so much," the brown-haired girl said. "Danke. Danke. You saved my little brother. You and the other boy. Thank you." She rested the baby's head on her shoulder.

"Are there a lot of those things around here?" I

managed to say through my gasping breath.

The girl smiled and shook her head. "Not so many. But the camp has its share of strange creatures. When we first came here, we called the camp 'the land that time forgot.' I think we've gotten more use to it now. You just have to watch your step. I should never have put little Hans down here alone. It was my fault."

The other kids crowded under the bleachers, carefully walking around the mangled bodies of the dead tarantulas, their mouths hanging open in wonder. Sonny pushed one of the dead spiders with the toe of his shoe.

"Thank you again," the brown-haired girl said. "I am Hannah Oudt."

"Ricky Parker. I'm new here. My dad's the new drilling supervisor."

"Ah. Perhaps he will get things moving on the rigs again. The last supervisor lost control of the men. A shame."

"You speak English," I said, a little puzzled.

Hannah laughed. "Of course. I had classes in English back in Heidelberg. And here? English is the language of oil." She shifted the baby on her hip. Little Hans had forgotten the attack of the tarantulas and was perfectly happy playing with loose strands of Hannah's hair.

Hannah had really deep brown eyes and really white teeth. And the little freckles across her nose were really cute. My best guess was she was about fifteen. And I'm telling you, the freckles were really cute.

"Welcome to the Creole Oil Camp," she smiled. "I

know the boys are pleased you are here. You are a fine player of the baseball. You will make the games more fun."

"Thanks."

"Come next Saturday. I will bring you a reward for saving little Hans."

I didn't know what to say.

Out past the bleachers, Romulo had hooked up with his Venezuelan buddies, and they were heading toward the outfield and the pasture beyond. Baseball was over for the day. He turned back and waved to me and then flashed one finger and then two and grinned.

I waved back and gave him the thumb and forefinger okay signal.

Then I turned back to Hannah Oudt and her really cute freckles.

《 6 》

I couldn't wait for the following Saturday. And it didn't have anything to do with baseball. It had to do with Hannah Oudt.

Hannah and her freckles and her smile had moved into my brain and kicked everything else out. Baseball, comics . . . see ya later. It was weird. The hours crept by. I couldn't wait to see her again.

Sunday crawled into Monday. Monday slogged slowly into Tuesday, which lasted about a month. Then Wednesday dawned and brought something I had totally forgotten about. With Hannah always on my mind, I had forgotten that Wednesday was the day Daddy wanted to take me out to the rig and show me why I had to leave my friends back in El Dorado and live in the "land that time forgot" as Hannah called the Creole Camp.

So Wednesday morning I found myself standing on the big rig in the middle of Lake Maracaibo.

"These are your triple drill centers, which are hydraulically operated. You have to have them to drill offshore," my father shouted above the deafening clanging and banging of the monstrous pumps.

"They're the only drill heads that can withstand the pressure."

Taking me out to the rig was a nice gesture on my father's part, but I have to make a confession. Machines bore me. God knows I'd tried to learn to like them and understand how they work. But I just didn't care.

Sometimes I could feel my father's disappointment in my lack of interest in machinery. He'd be taking a radio apart at the kitchen table and call me in and show me the baker tubes and how they fit right next to the receiving cables or something like that. He'd be all excited about sharing this stuff with me, but then his face would fall when he realized I wasn't even listening. My mind had just wandered off somewhere else.

I couldn't help it. I loved comic books and baseball and fishing with Billy Tom and drinking sodas down at Mr. Webber's drugstore back home. But how machines worked, what all the little parts were, where they fit, and why they did what they did? My brain pulled a disappearing act when Daddy started talking about it.

And because I was the way I was, I could feel an invisible wall going up between my father and me. I hated the wall, but there seemed to be no way to tear it down. My father had no interest in baseball. None. He thought baseball was a waste of time. How you gonna tear that wall down? Especially with all the rage I still had inside of me about having to leave El Dorado.

Daddy could talk all he wanted about duty and war, but I knew deep inside of me that he made me and Mama move to a god-awful oil camp in the middle of nowhere so he could quit doing small appliance repair and get back on an oil rig. Daddy wasn't fooling me for a minute. So the wall grew higher and higher, and the more Daddy told me about machines the more I hated them.

"Up there near the top of the rig are the valve caps."

I managed a nod.

"Ricky, lad. How are you?" Uncle Harry crossed the narrow walkway to the platform where my father was teaching me the glories of oil-rig machinery. "Welcome aboard." He winked at me, letting me know he understood my situation with my dad and the machinery. What a great guy. He just automatically knew stuff.

"Thanks."

"The number nine rod containers need to be replaced, Ches," Uncle Harry said to my father.

My father grinned, fascinated by the very thought of rod containers.

"We also need to get some of the natives to rotate the lower cables. All it takes is muscle."

"I'll get 'em right on it." My father had his pipe securely clamped between his teeth. All around us the oil-rig workers were hard at their jobs, moving wires and cables and climbing the sides of the rig and climbing back down.

Off in the distance, I saw a small motorboat heading for the rig. The lake was calm and the white-capped waves lapped at the rig supports below us. Because of the pounding and clanking of the machines on the derrick, I couldn't hear the approaching boat. Watching the little vehicle dock at the rig was like watching a silent movie.

I recognized Mr. Taggert in the rear of the boat. He had on a blue work shirt, khaki trousers, and red suspenders. A crumpled fedora sat tilted back on his head. He wore a sour look.

"Time to get busy." Uncle Harry laughed, nodding toward Taggert.

"I reckon." Daddy smiled.

Daddy spent the next hour giving Mr. Taggert a tour of the rig. The company supervisor looked less than thrilled to see me on the job, so I kept my distance while they walked and climbed all over the oil derrick.

I was glad to see Mr. Taggert. Otherwise I'd have to try to pay attention to Daddy's descriptions of cranks and cranes and cables and bolts and screws and drill bits and the like.

Mr. Taggert stopped from time to time and asked the derrick hands about one thing or another. I thought he was rude to some of the workers, snapping at them if they didn't answer his questions fast enough, but the men just answered as best they could and went back to their jobs.

At lunchtime, Daddy and I found a place on the edge of the platform with a small group of workers who were eating their lunches out of black pails just like ours.

Mama had fixed us bologna sandwiches and sugar cookies wrapped in wax paper. I had milk in my thermos. Daddy had black coffee.

It was hard to talk over the roar of the drilling machines, and for a few minutes, nobody said anything while we ate our lunch.

"There was a company guy at the baseball field the other day," I said over the roar of the engines. "He had a shotgun. The fellows told me he was there to protect us from the local Indians."

My father shook his head. "I don't think you have anything to worry about on that count. The Indians that used to live on the lake are peaceful now. Have been for quite a spell. Somebody in the company is overreacting. The camp's a safe place. I wouldn't have brought you and your mama down here if it wasn't."

I wasn't so sure about that.

Daddy took a bite of his bologna sandwich and washed it down with coffee. We sat for a while and listened to the steady clinking and clanking of the oil rig, which probably sounded like Mozart to my father.

"What do the Germans do in the camp?" I asked during a lull in the machine noise. I had proudly told Mama and Daddy about the tarantulas at the baseball field. Mama was concerned I might have gotten spider poison on me and rushed me into the shower while she fussed at Daddy for taking us to such a godforsaken place. I didn't tell them about the German kids and Hannah. I mean your folks don't have to know everything. Right?

"The Germans?" Daddy looked up from his sandwich. "Oh, most of 'em are petroleum engineers or geologists. They work back at the administration building. They seem to be a nice enough lot. We don't see much of them out here on the rigs."

"Do you know one named Oudt?"

"Dr. Oudt? Yeah. I've met him. A quiet fellow. Good engineer. Been with the company a lot of years. Solid man."

I washed down a bite of sandwich with some milk from the thermos top. "You think he's one of those Nazi fellows?"

My father looked puzzled. "I dunno. I suppose they all are to some degree. Oudt and I never talked about the situation in Germany. Most engineers don't care much for politics. I hope he's not a Nazi. You know what I think about that bunch of thugs."

"Are some of the other Germans in the camp real Nazis?"

"I hope not. There are not that many Germans down here anymore, and they tend to just do their job and mind their own business. We're not at war with Germany so I guess it doesn't matter that much."

It mattered to me. Since last Saturday and the tarantula attack I couldn't think about much else besides Hannah Oudt. I tried my best not to think about her, but every time I'd get into a comic and Billy Batson would turn into Captain Marvel and go after the bad guys, all of a sudden Hannah Oudt's face would pop into my mind. Just like that. I couldn't wait for next Saturday when I could see her again.

But if her family was a bunch of Nazis who loved Hitler and wanted to kill all the English people and the poor Poles and Danes and Frenchmen and stuff like that, it made what I was feeling kinda tough. I just couldn't imagine somebody as pretty and nice as Hannah being a Nazi. But you never knew. Germans were Germans. But German or not, I couldn't get Hannah Oudt out of my mind.

Daddy changed the subject and started rambling on about how the big cables in the center of the derrick kept the drills from running out of control. I stayed with him for a couple of minutes and then Shazam! Hannah Oudt took over my brain.

"Right. Big cables." I tried to sound interested, but believe me, it was a stretch.

"I use those machines over there to make sure the oil and gas doesn't come out too fast. Uncle Harry helps me in that department. He's one of the best blowout specialists in the business."

"Wow." I didn't know what else to say.

We were just about finished with lunch when Mr. Taggert climbed the ladder up to our platform. Uncle Harry followed close behind.

"Mr. Ches, we need to get moving on replacing those cables," Mr. Taggert said. "I want to make sure that's done before I head back to shore. Harry says we need new ones, but I reckon those retreads will work just fine for a while."

"Yes, sir," my father said without much conviction.

Down in the corner of the rig, just at sea level, the men started resetting the big cables. A half dozen Venezuelan workers came over to help out. They all needed a haircut and looked dark and sullen. Their shirts were splattered with grease and stained with sweat. One of them looked a little like Romulo and I wondered if the man might be his father.

Uncle Harry lined up the Venezuelan workers behind the giant turrets that held the cables. The natives would hold the cable like men in a big game of tug-of-war, while the American guys rethreaded the new cables on the band wheel's axle. Everybody on both lines was grunting, straining, and sweating. Uncle Harry quickly made some adjustments with a wrench.

Daddy stood off to one side with Mr. Taggert and gnawed on his pipe stem, while Mr. Taggert patted his foot impatiently. "I haven't got all day, Mr. Ches," he said. "Let's be quick about this."

"Yes, sir." Daddy walked over to the line. "Hurry it up, Harry. Quick as you can."

Uncle Harry frowned. Then he moved to the front and, pulling at the cable, tried to hook it around this giant spindle. "Hold steady back there," he called over his shoulder. The man who looked like Romulo yelled something in Spanish to the men behind him.

"Uno, dos, tres . . . now," Uncle Harry yelled.

Muscles bulged and the men behind him grunted and strained.

The cable slipped over the spindle.

"Good work," Daddy said. "One more and we've got it."

"Just be quick about it," Mr. Taggert said, glancing at his pocket watch.

Uncle Harry hooked up the second cable and the Venezuelans again strained to hold it in place. "All right, here we go," he called. "Uno, dos, tres . . . now."

The men grunted and strained, but this time Uncle

Harry couldn't get the cable over the top of the spindle. He tried and tried but somehow it just wouldn't fit.

"Let me give you a hand, Harry. You help the men hold and I'll slip the cable.

"Thanks, Ches." Uncle Harry's face was bathed in sweat.

Daddy took Uncle Harry's place and Uncle Harry moved back to help pull the cable tight.

"Here we go men, one more time. Uno, dos, tres . . . hold her tight."

Daddy grabbed the cable and hoisted the line up and over the top of the spindle.

Then something happened. The thick cable slipped forward. Daddy's right hand was pulled under the cable as it hooked over the spindle. My father screamed in agony. His pipe fell out of his mouth and clattered on the platform. At first he couldn't get his hand out from under the cable and blood streamed down his wrist and over his sleeve.

I froze. I had never seen my father hurt. I didn't know what to do.

"Pull back, men!" Uncle Harry yelled. "Hard as you can. Now! Pull!"

The cable came back just enough to let Daddy pull out his hand. His flesh was ripped open across the knuckles. With the cable secure, the men let go.

"Ah!!" Daddy staggered backward, shaking the hand and then cradling it with his other hand. His face went pale.

I fought back tears. Terror gripped my gut and acid filled my throat. I choked back vomit. Daddy's hand looked horrible.

"You stupid fools!" Mr. Taggert lunged forward and shoved the Venezuelan who looked like Romulo. The other men backed up in fear. "You worthless . . . you're all fired! You hear me!"

"Mr. Taggert, sir," Uncle Harry said. "It wasn't their fault. The men did the best they could. It's a hard job to hold the cable back for that long."

"Shut up, Kramer! This isn't your concern." Mr. Taggert whirled on the men. "All of you get off this rig—now! Pack your gear and be on the ferry to Maracaibo by sundown. Pick up your pay at the office on your way out." He shoved the man in front again.

The man turned to his friends. He was shaking. He spoke to his buddies in Spanish. A couple of them glared at Mr. Taggert, snarling with raw hatred, making no effort to hide their feelings.

"My god, Chester, how bad is it?" Mr. Taggert put his hand on Daddy's shoulder. "You're pale as a ghost. You must be going into shock. Let me have a look at that hand."

I peered over Mr. Taggert's shoulder. Daddy's hand looked like a bloody piece of hamburger. Dread ran crazy in my head. My hands shook.

Daddy leaned against the platform railing. His hand dripped blood in puddles on the floor of the deck.

"Lord, I hope you don't lose your fingers," Mr. Taggert said. "You can ride back to shore in my launch. I'll take you to the infirmary."

Daddy nodded. His lips were set in a thin line.

"Kramer, get those miserable . . . lazy . . . just get

them out of here right now. They're all fired. Every last one of them."

Uncle Harry bit down hard on his lower lip and whirled around. The veins lunged against the restraint of his neck. He was beyond furious.

Suddenly my dad's knees buckled and he sank to the deck. Uncle Harry and I grabbed him. Daddy's eyes rolled back in his head and terror gripped my heart. I felt like I was gonna faint and realized I'd been holding my breath for a long time

≪ 7 ≫

Mr. Taggert parked in front of the hospital.

The company infirmary was housed in a brown one-story stucco building across the road from the British compound. Palm trees lined the walkway to the front door. The compound across the road was deserted. Since the war started, the British workers had all gone home to help with the war effort.

My father's skin had turned a waxy gray color by the time we got to the infirmary. He was shaking all over. We got out of the car and I put my arm around his waist. He leaned on me as we hobbled up the walkway to the front door. We had to stop halfway there so my father could catch his breath.

Daddy was a brave man and always had been but that day he had lost a lot of blood and looked near dead by the time we got to the infirmary.

Right after we got inside the door, Daddy lost his balance and I guided him to a nearby bench. He sat hunched on the bench, clutching his injured hand at his side. His face turned pale.

"See! See what you get for making us move down here! See what you get for making us leave El Dorado!"

I couldn't stand it. I couldn't stop myself. Everything came rushing out. "You made me leave all my friends, everything I loved. And why? For your stupid oil rigs? And now, and now, you might even lose your fingers!" I stopped, struggling to take a breath while glaring at him."

Daddy slowly raised his head. "I'm sorry, Son. I know this has been hard on you and your Mama. You can't imagine how sorry I am."

One look at the sadness in my father's eyes and I hated myself for what I'd said. Daddy was hurting and I had piled on him. I sat down on the bench beside him and draped my arm around his shoulder. I didn't want to say anything else. I just wanted to stop myself from making matters worse by sobbing like a little baby.

At that moment, Mr. Taggert stormed through the front door of the hospital. "You want me to fetch the missus?" he asked.

Daddy's body sagged against me. "No. I imagine she's over at the club, deep in her bridge and bourbon by now. No. Ricky and I can handle it. Thank you though."

Mr. Taggert nodded. "Suit yourself."

I had never heard Daddy mention Mama's drinking to anyone. Hearing him say the words out loud took me by surprise.

Daddy struggled to his feet and nodded at Mr. Taggert. Then we slowly shuffled into the infirmary together.

The inside of the hospital smelled like disinfectant and bug spray. A big ceiling fan in the lobby instantly made the hot day more bearable. Daddy clutched his injured hand close to his body. He didn't say anything else about my outburst.

The nurse at the front desk was a stern looking woman with a slight mustache. Her dull mousey hair was tied in a tight bun. At first she scowled at us like we were interrupting her, but after she took one look at Daddy's hand, she ran to find a doctor. Uncle Harry had located some old towels on the rig and wrapped up Daddy's injury, but the white towels were soaked dark crimson by the time we got to the front desk.

The doctor meandered out to the lobby in a couple of minutes. He was a short man with slicked-back thinning hair, a cigarette dangling from the corner of his mouth and a three-day growth of beard. He winced when he saw Daddy's mangled hand.

Back in a cramped little office, the doctor laid my father's hand out on a table covered in a white sheet and cleaned the wound with careful, gentle strokes. Daddy grimaced each time the doctor touched his injured hand. I leaned against the back wall, my arms folded across my chest, trying to look like I wasn't scared.

"So what d'you think, Doc?" Daddy sounded more like his old self and I felt waves of relief wash over me.

"I think another quarter inch or so and you'd have lost all your fingers," the doctor said without taking the cigarette out of his mouth. "You're a lucky man, Mr. Parker. I reckon I can sew you back up. You'll be good as new after a while. But that hand won't be much good to you for a few weeks."

Daddy nodded.

I reached into my pocket and pulled out Daddy's pipe that I had retrieved from the platform on the derrick before we got on the boat.

Daddy grinned when he saw the pipe. "Thanks, Ricky." He parked the pipe stem in its usual place in the corner of his mouth. Then he winked at me. I tried to smile back, but it didn't work.

"I need to go find some thicker sutures," the doctor said. "I've got some thin ones here, but if I use them you'll have a pretty bad scar. I'll be back in a minute." He got up and ambled through the open door.

Daddy relaxed and gnawed on his pipe stem. Knowing he wasn't going to lose his fingers seemed to have made him feel much better. "I'm sorry we picked today to take you out on the rig," he said. "That sort of thing doesn't happen often. It's a shame you had to see it."

"It's okay. I'm just glad you're gonna be all right."

"Working the derricks can be dangerous work."

"Not like fixing radios and toasters back in El Dorado, huh?"

My tone made Daddy's eyebrows shoot up. "Well, no," he stammered. "But that's part of why Harry and I like working the rigs. Sure it's tough work, but at the end of the day you feel like you did something important. The danger is just part of the job."

"Why did Mr. Taggert talk that way to the Venezuelans?" I had to change the subject before all the rage inside me came rushing out again. "Uncle Harry said it wasn't their fault."

Daddy shook his head. "It wasn't. Those men did the best they could. There really wasn't any reason for Taggert to speak to them like that. Let alone fire them. They sure didn't deserve that."

"Mr. Taggert was pretty hateful," I said.

"Some men, and Ed Taggert is one of them, just have hate deep down inside of them. It's hard to explain. You remember how some of the white people back home felt about the black folks. Just hated 'em because of who they were. I reckon old man Taggert feels that way about the natives down here."

What my father was talking about was this thing the Ku Klux Klan did back in El Dorado a couple of years ago. A bunch of white men got all liquored up and put on these silly looking sheets like robes and then put pillow cases with eye holes cut in them over their heads and got together out in Elmer Baylen's back pasture. They set a giant cross on fire and sang a bunch of hymns.

I was spending the night at Elmer's house. We did that every once in a while so we could stay up late and swap comics and eat oatmeal raisin cookies and talk about everything under the sun. That night I was kinda hoping Elmer would open the bathroom door, so I could see Ruby naked again.

But before that happened, we heard the Klan out in the pasture and saw the flames leaping into the summer night. Elmer and I ran out the back door before Mrs. Baylen knew what we were up to, and we found us a spot in a grove of oak trees on a little hill that overlooked the pasture where the Klan was gathered.

We stayed in the shadows and watched the whole sorry thing. It was awful. The Klansmen lit torches and marched around in a circle, chanting something that sounded like a foreign language.

Then three cars drove across the pasture to where the Klan was carrying on. The cars' headlights cast eerie shadows over the firelit pasture. I recognized Charlie Jackson's father's old Ford and Ben Livemore's daddy's Chevy. Charlie and Ben were a year ahead of me at school and played on the baseball team. I didn't know the other car.

A bunch of men piled out of the cars like clowns in the little car at the circus. Only these clowns were dressed in sheets and pillowcases. They opened the trunk of the Ford and drug out these two black men. The black men had their hands tied behind them and white handkerchiefs blindfolding their eyes. They were both so scared they were shaking all over. One of 'em looked like he had peed his pants. I didn't recognize him, but the other one looked like Jake the yardman who cuts lawns in town. He was a real friendly fellow. He always waved to me when I went by on my bike. I always waved back.

The Klansmen tied the black men up to a pair of posts near the fire. Then everybody got quiet while one of the Klansmen said a bunch of stuff about America being a white man's country and black folks knowing their place. I think that was Charlie Jackson's father. It was a real hateful speech.

Then another Klansman got a bullwhip out of the trunk of the Chevy and proceeded to beat both of the black men with it. The whip ripped the shirts off their backs and then ripped off some big strips of skin. All the other Klansmen cheered and clapped with each blow.

Elmer and I got scared and ran all the way back to the Baylen's house. Neither one of us slept a wink that night. The next day the news was all over town. I never told Mama and Daddy what we saw that night but I had nightmares for a couple of weeks. Daddy heard about what the Klan did, and I overheard him tell Mama that it was a terrible crime those fellows acted that way.

Standing in the doctor's office at the Creole Camp infirmary, I wondered if Mr. Taggert had been one of the hooded Klansmen that night, seeing as how he was so full of hate.

Hate was hate no matter where you aimed it, but somehow Mr. Taggert's outburst at the Venezuelan workers seemed even worse.

"But, Daddy, this is the Venezuelans' country." My voice went up a couple of octaves. "It's their oil. Mr. Taggert shouldn't treat them like that."

My father looked surprised. "Well, you're right, Son. We are in Venezuela and we are pumping Venezuelan oil. But the law says the oil belongs to the company. The Creole Company pays the Venezuelan government for the right to take the oil and I don't reckon the natives could get it out of the lake without the company. But still, you're right. In the final analysis it is their oil."

"It doesn't seem fair," I said.

"No it doesn't. But listen, Ricky. Do me a favor.

Don't be talking that way back in the camp. This is a tricky question. Folks take for granted that we should be here pumping the oil out of Venezuela, making money for the company."

"I have some bad news, Mr. Parker." The doctor swept back into the room, the cigarette still dangling from his mouth. "We don't seem to have any of the heavy duty sutures on hand right now. No pun intended. You know how it is. But we need to sew up your wound immediately. Can you live with what might be a bad scar across your knuckles?"

A puzzled frown crossed Daddy's face. "Reckon I got no choice, Doc," he said. "Sew her up as best you can and I'll be mighty grateful. But I reckon Creole needs to get the hospital resupplied right quick though. Some of the boys out on the rig told me you were all out of iodine and aspirin the other day. That's unacceptable." My father let out a sigh. "I could have sworn Taggert told me not too long ago that the hospital was fully stocked." Daddy shook his head. "I guess the company can't see after every little thing, but the boys need proper medication."

"Right you are, Mr. Parker," the doctor forced a smile. "Here, I brought you a little something that's better'n most of the company's medicine. I'll deaden your hand, but a shot of this should make the suturing go smoother." He pulled a silver flask out of his jacket pocket.

Daddy beamed. "Just what the doctor ordered."

I let out a big sigh. Suddenly I knew everything was gonna be all right.

Only somehow it never was.

« 8 »

The next Saturday I headed over to the baseball field early. Daddy had stayed home from work because his hand was bothering him, and Mama felt like she needed to stay home with him, which meant she was going to miss her bridge game at the club. She was cranky and spent most of the morning dreaming up stupid little chores for me to do—clean off the front porch, mow the front yard, shell a bunch of stupid peas she had picked up at the company store.

So I left early that afternoon for the baseball field. I wanted out of the house for sure, but mostly I wanted to play baseball . . . and see Hannah Oudt.

When I got to the field, Sonny and Will Cole were already there, playing a lazy game of catch down the third base line. They let me join them. Sonny didn't say anything about the tarantulas and how he chickened out and wouldn't help me and Romulo. I decided to just let it go.

After a while Romulo and his buddies showed up and warmed up way out in the outfield. The guard with the shotgun appeared a few minutes later and a few other guys drifted in and started playing catch.

Then the two German boys showed up. By themselves. No Hannah. My brain dissolved into a weird stew of anger, disappointment, and frustration.

We divided up into teams and started the game. It must have been Will's turn to pitch instead of Sonny and little Will had a good fastball. Better than Sonny's I thought. Sonny played short. He was a better shortstop than a pitcher. An American guy named Bobby pitched for the Yankees. Romulo played center field.

It was a good game. Bobby was no Walter Johnson and the Cards got a lot of hits. That made the game fun. I blasted a double off of Will and slid in under the tag at second. When I stood up and dusted myself off, Romulo grinned at me from out in center field and gave me the okay sign. I grinned back.

The next inning, Sonny hit a single, but I threw him out trying to steal second on the next pitch.

As I was putting the mask back on, I glanced behind me and saw Hannah and her friend heading for the bleachers. Hannah had on a starched yellow blouse and a white skirt. Her hair was all shiny and wavy. She was carrying a small basket looped through her arm.

There was no sign of little Hans.

The girls sat in the bleachers and the game started again. A guy named Max hit a single. Will came up and took a pitch. On the next pitch Max took off for second. I grabbed the ball and rifled it toward second. Instead I rifled it right into center field. It was the worst throw I'd ever made in my life. I stole a quick glance over at Hannah. She smiled at me.

I came up to bat the next inning and struck out on

three straight fastballs. I was a good hitter and had faced a lot tougher pitchers than Will, but something was wrong. I couldn't concentrate. All I could do was steal little glances at Hannah and then quickly look away so she wouldn't think I was looking at her. Once she showed up at the field, my whole game went south. It was pathetic.

The Yankees beat the Cards something like 21–18.

The sun was sinking slowly over the horizon, and the crickets or whatever they were started chirping like crazy. The shadows from the school stretched over the field. The guys waved and headed back for the American compound. Romulo and his buddies disappeared.

I drifted over to the bleachers with the two German boys.

"Hi," I said as I approached Hannah.

"Hi yourself." She sounded just like an American girl. The weather was humid and Hannah had a thin bead of sweat across her upper lip. "You boys can't seem to get enough of your baseball."

"Greatest game in the world," I said.

Hannah smiled. I felt dizzy. There was something about her. When I looked at her, everything and everybody else just blurred into the background.

"How is Hans?" I asked.

"Fit and fiddle," Hannah said. "No worse for the wear. But meine Mutter decided no more baseball for the tike."

"Probably a good idea."

"And," Hannah said, "I brought you a thank-you

gift for saving my little brother." She indicated the basket in her lap.

"You didn't have to do that."

"Is my pleasure," she said. "Is a strudel. With the apples and the sugar. I made it myself. I hope you like it."

"I've never had strudel." I wasn't even sure what strudel was. But if Hannah made it, I was sure it was the best-tasting thing in the world.

"Sit and have a bite."

I flopped down on the bleachers beside her.

She reached into the basket and brought out the strudel, which was wrapped up in wax paper. After opening up the paper, Hannah broke off a bit of the gooey pastry and offered it to me. I popped the flakey stuff into my mouth, and I'm here to tell you, Hannah Oudt's strudel is what the angels are gonna serve the first day you get to heaven. I was probably hungry after playing ball all afternoon, but trust me, the strudel was unbelievable.

So was the rest of the afternoon.

We sat on the bleachers and shared the strudel, gobbling up every delicious crumb. Hannah's friend, Mindi, said she was going to walk home with the other two German boys. Hannah and I sat in the bleachers and talked for a while and then she ask me to walk her home.

If she had asked me, I would have walked through fire.

We wandered across the fields that fronted the jungle behind the camp.

"School will be starting soon," Hannah said. "How old are you?"

"I turn thirteen next week."

"Ah. You will be in the last group. Next year you'll have to go back to the states. The school doesn't go any higher."

"What about you?"

"I finished the school last year. This year my Papa will tutor me at home. He doesn't want to go back to Heidelberg with the war on. He says families should not separate during the time of war. He loves mathematics and physics and chemistry. Strange things for a girl to study, ja? Strange but not uninteresting. What do you like to study?"

"Me? Study? Gee, I dunno." I didn't like to study anything, but I knew that wasn't a good answer. So I took a blind shot. "I always did pretty well in history," I said.

"A good subject."

We crossed the field and stopped and played around in the giant pipes, listening to our voices echo though the giant concrete cylinders, shouting silly things and laughing when our silliness came back to us. There were no dragons in the pipes that afternoon.

"How long have you been at the camp?" I asked as we started walking again.

"Four years now," she said. "Since I was ten. In some ways the camp is the only home I've ever really known. Before we came to the camp, Papa worked for the Royal Dutch company in Turkey and then in Persia. I hardly remember our home in Heidelberg."

"In Germany?"

"Ja. It's a beautiful little town with a large university. I remember the university students who came to our house. They were so serious. Papa was their professor and they came to talk so earnestly about engineering, geology, about oil production and such. The students were always so polite. I don't remember much else."

We could hear monkeys screeching deep in the jungle. "Do you like living in the camp?"

Hannah paused and looked out toward the thick jungle about a hundred yards from where we were walking. "Not so much anymore," she said. "At first there were many Germans in the camp. They were good workers, educated in the engineering, and the company sought them out. There were many of us and we had parties at the Club. We got together and sang German songs. The men drank the beer until their faces turned red, and they laughed and remembered the good times from the Fatherland."

"Sounds like fun."

"Oh it was. Then . . ." Hannah's voice grew distant. Then she got quiet.

I decided not to say anything.

"Then," she finally said, letting out a deep breath. "The war came. The horrible, terrible war. And it was not so much fun to live in the camp. There were still English workers back then. They refused to work with the Deutchers. They spit on the Germans. There were awful fights between the men. Then the English left."

"Was it better then?"

"Nein. Many, many of our German friends were called home to the Fatherland. Only a handful of us remain. My papa is a valuable geologist. The company promised to raise his pay if he would stay. He agreed. He doesn't like the Führer. He doesn't like the war. He loves geology. So he remains. Some of the others are different. The younger workers think Herr Hitler is the future of the Fatherland."

I picked up a rock and pegged it in the general direction of the jungle.

"But now life in the camp is hard," Hannah went on. "We no longer go to the Club or to the parties. We stay to ourselves. But there are so few of us. The Americans distrust us. The boys only allow Karl and Johann to play the baseball because they so badly need players."

She was right about that.

Hannah grew silent and we walked on for a while. The quiet didn't feel bad at all. It was just fun to be with her.

"And where are you from in America?" Hannah asked in her beautiful German-accented singsong voice. "I know New York and Chicago. And Milwaukee. In Wisconsin."

"El Dorado, in Arkansas," I said proudly.

"El Dorado? For real?"

"Sure."

"Ah. El Dorado is the mythical city of gold."

"Not the one I'm from."

"No. El Dorado is a legendary city. The famous English explorer Sir Walter Raleigh looked for El

Dorado right here in Venezuela."

News to me. "And I left El Dorado to come to Venezuela," I grinned.

Hannah smiled back. "Ja. To be sure."

Then we walked along the path for a while, smiling at nothing.

"There is the German compound," she said as we approached the back of a couple rows of houses. The houses were all recently painted and had green shutters and flower boxes and trimmed lawns. "Now it is, what you Americans call a 'ghost town.' Most of the houses are empty. Just a handful at the end of the lane. Is not a good way to live. It's a lonely way to live."

"I bet."

"But you are somehow different than the others. You will talk to me."

"I . . . like . . . talking . . . to . . . you." I sounded like an idiot.

"Come!" Hannah took my hand. "I show you one more thing." She broke into a trot and I followed along behind, holding on to her hand, never wanting to let go.

We ran past a few more houses and an open field. On the far side of the field, we pulled up on the bank of a big creek. The muddy water was down and brown rocks poked up all over the creek bed.

"Look over there." Hannah dropped my hand and pointed across the creek at a row of battered shanty houses. The places were falling in, porches sagging dangerously, exposed weathered boards, dirt yards, scrawny chickens scratching at the earth, a couple of pigs rooting in the brush.

"This is what Creole thinks of the people of Venezuela." A sudden anger filled Hannah's voice. "This is the native camp. You and I cannot go there. Ever. The natives are beneath our contempt. Even Romulo and his friends. The best baseball players in all of Lake Maracaibo. They come and play and then must return to this." Her arm swept the air indicating the sordid native camp. "The company comes and takes their oil and treats them like this."

"I know." I quickly told her the story of what had happened to Daddy and how Mr. Taggert had fired all the native workers on the spot even though they hadn't done anything wrong.

"But you know what, my friend?" Hannah said after she heard the story. "It is the same the world over."

"What d'you mean?"

"Everywhere people find other people to look down on. To scorn. To blame. Everywhere. In my country it's the Jews. In yours, the Negroes. Here the Europeans and the Americans come and turn on the Venezuelans. You see what I mean? It's everywhere. Like a dark stain on all of mankind. You see?"

I did. And for a long, long time the sadness of what Hannah showed me that afternoon plagued me like a ghost.

I walked her back to the German compound, and we stood outside the gate for a while, not talking, not wanting the afternoon to end. I took Hannah's hand and held it for a while. She didn't pull away.

"They're starting the Sunday night movies again

tomorrow," Hannah said in a low voice. "On the tennis courts behind the bachelor barracks. I haven't been in a long time. I'd like to go tomorrow and see the Bogart picture. Will you be going?"

"Sure. Yeah. I guess." I hadn't heard about the movies.

Hannah smiled. "You might as well go. The company takes the price of the ticket out of your father's pay. Please go. We could sit together. I wouldn't be afraid to go if I knew you would be there."

"Then I'll be there." I gave her hand a squeeze.

The next night Hannah and I went to the movies. We thrilled to the exploits of Humphrey Bogart and laughed at the Mickey Mouse cartoon that preceded the film, and afterwards we took a walk in the Venezuelan moonlight.

And that's when we found the dead body.

≪ 9 ≫

The movie on the tennis court was fun. The court was located between the Club and the bachelor's barracks and the company put up a portable screen at one end of the court and rows of slatted wooden folding chairs facing the screen. There was no net and weeds peeked up through cracks in the asphalt. I guess tennis wasn't big with oil workers.

Some of the women came to the Club early and popped mountains of popcorn, filled brown lunch sacks, and gave everybody a bag. They sold bottles of Coca-Cola with a little yellow straw for a nickel.

Mama and Daddy went with me to the show. My father's hand was still all wrapped up in a gauze bandage, but he felt better and seemed more like his old self. Sitting there waiting for the picture show to start, Mama held Daddy's other hand, her fingers laced in his fingers like the high school kids at the movies back in El Dorado.

I wore my best blue shirt and a pair of black slacks. I even polished my shoes and put some Brylcreem in my hair.

I met Hannah by the table behind the club where

the ladies were passing out the popcorn. A couple of the popcorn ladies gave Hannah a strange look, but I didn't think much of it at the time.

Hannah had on a white blouse and a black skirt. She even had on a little makeup. Her hair was pulled back with a barrette, and she looked like a princess in a fairy tale. We found seats near the back and munched popcorn and sipped Cokes.

A couple of rows in front of us, I saw Uncle Harry and the doctor from the infirmary sitting with a couple of Uncle Harry's buddies from the bachelor barracks. The doctor had a cigarette dangling from the side of his mouth. The men were all eating popcorn and yukking it up, having a great time. I guess Uncle Harry hadn't had time to change clothes from the rig. His shoes and pants were covered with dirt and mud and his shaved head was pearled with sweat.

The evening was warm. At first there was still a little light and a lot of moths frantically circling the light from the projector, but by the time Mickey and Goofy and Pluto finished their part of the show, darkness blanketed the tennis court and Humphrey Bogart looked just as good on the portable screen as he did back at the Rialto Theater in El Dorado.

On the screen, Bogart and his valiant crew were battling a raging Arctic blizzard. Polar bears and seals stood on the glacier staring in wonder at Bogart's icebound ship. The thick falling snow made it hard to see anything. It was a heck of a storm.

Yet all around Hannah and me, crickets chirped and the scent of magnolias filled the air. Above us the tropical sky twinkled with stars.

A couple of mangy dogs slipped onto the court and barked at the polar bears.

After the movie I volunteered to walk Hannah back to the German compound. She flashed a shy smile and said okay. My heart skipped a couple of beats.

As we walked away from the tennis court, we could hear the sounds of laughter and talking coming from the patio behind the Club. Movie night at the Creole Camp was like a party. Everyone hung around to socialize when the film ended. Everyone except Hannah and me.

We took our time going back to the German compound, circling around behind the deserted British housing and taking the dirt path that ran between the compounds and the giant pipes.

A harvest moon sat high and bright in the sky, casting shadows everywhere, making the pipes look spooky in the moonlight. Hannah laughed when I said the pipes looked like abandoned space ships. She said we'd better be careful and watch out for the creepy creatures that came on the ships.

The tropical night was alive with sound—the shrill chirping of the crickets and cicadas' endless nocturnal song. Beyond the pipes the jungle creatures joined the chorus. On the other side of the narrow path I could even hear beetles scratching the trunks of the trees. Way off, far beyond the camp, I heard an animal's high-pitched shriek.

As we walked along, I was working up my courage to kiss Hannah when we got to the gate of the

German compound. Kiss her on the lips. I'd never kissed a girl before. I was far more scared of the prospect than I was of any space monsters, but I was determined to try. Until I talked myself out of it. Then I talked myself back into it. I was gonna do it. I was gonna kiss Hannah Oudt. Or maybe not.

Just about the time I had worked myself into a kissing frenzy, Hannah stopped in the middle of the path and pointed toward the pipe nearest the road. The creek meandered just behind the pipe, and I could hear the bubbling of the creek water, amplified through the giant concrete cylinder.

"Look over there. In the pipe. Shoes. Ja. Shoes." Hannah grabbed my arm. "See. There. Oh, mein Gott. Ricky. There's someone in the pipe."

I looked where she was pointing. Sure enough, a pair of legs were sticking out of the pipe. They weren't moving. Everything was quiet and still. Except for my heart, which suddenly was pounding ninety miles an hour.

"Go and see," Hannah whispered.

Go and see? Me? She wanted me to walk over to that creepy dark pipe entrance and look in where those legs were sticking out. I might have been brave enough to kiss Hannah, but I wasn't so sure about this new proposition.

But I would rather have wrestled rattlesnakes or alligators than have Hannah Oudt think I was chicken. Would Humphrey Bogart go look in the pipe? Tom Mix? Captain Marvel? Did I have a choice?

I left Hannah standing on the path and made my

way to the pipe entrance. The moon was like a monstrous lightbulb in the sky, and I could clearly see into the pipe.

The body belonged to Mr. Taggert. He was lying on his back, his unseeing eyes wide open like he was staring at the top of the pipe. His glasses were all whopperjawed across his face. His white shirt was covered with dark reddish spots. You didn't need to be Bulldog Drummond to figure out the front of his shirt was soaked in dried blood and the blood came from his throat, which was neatly sliced open from ear to ear.

I fought a quick war with my stomach, which wanted to heave in the worst way.

"What is it, Ricky?" Hannah came up behind me.

"No, don't come over . . ." I was too late.

Hannah peered over my shoulder. "Oh, mein Gott." She crossed herself.

I just stood there, my legs too heavy to move. "It's Mr. Taggert," I said. "My father's drilling manager."

"He is dead, ja?"

"I've . . . I've never seen a dead person. But, yeah, I'm pretty sure he's dead. Look at his eyes."

"Oh, how awful."

The creek bubbled on behind the pipe and the noise brought me out of my trance. "Hannah. We've got to get out of here. Whoever did this could still be hiding in one of these pipes. Or over in the trees. Or anywhere."

"Ja. We go for help."

We backed away from the body, turned, and then took off sprinting back the way we'd come. Hannah was a fast runner even in the sandy, muddy soil. Our arms were pumping and Hannah's skirt bellowed behind her.

Hannah and I ran all the way back to the Club, where a few people were sitting around the picnic table having drinks and finishing off the last of the movie popcorn. I didn't recognize any of them.

"Help . . . come quick!" I was sucking serious wind from running so hard. "Mr. Taggert . . . in the pipe . . . dead. Please come . . . quick."

The rest of the night was a blur. I led three men back to the pipe and Mr. Taggert's body. After I showed them the corpse, one of the men walked me back to the Club. My father was there, waiting for me. I guess somebody took Hannah back to the German compound because I didn't see her anymore that night.

Back at our house I was a little nuts, talking to beat the band. Daddy sat at the kitchen table and smoked his pipe, listening intently, willing to let me tell the story again and again. Mama just nodded a lot, while she absentmindedly shredded Kleenex.

Finally, I ran out of gas, went to my room, and fell on my bed in all my clothes.

When I woke up in the morning, someone had taken off my shoes and covered me up with the bedspread. Mama fixed eggs, bacon, and toast, and I ate and ate. Then Daddy said he and I had to go over to the Club and talk to some people.

We got to the Club around noon. There were a couple of people milling around in the foyer, but clearly what was happening was happening in the main room. The card tables were pushed back against the wall and the bar was deserted. A small metal desk had been set up in one corner, and a man in shirtsleeves and a tie sat behind the desk talking to a couple of Daddy's crewmen.

The man stood up as we approached the desk. "Mr. Ches, how are you, sir?"

Daddy and the man shook hands.

"Ricky, this is John Long. He's the head of security for the camp."

Long held out his hand and I shook it. His grip almost broke my fingers. He was a thickset man, a little older than Daddy, with dark hair going gray at the temples and tiny ferret eyes.

"Mr. Long used to be with the Dallas Police Department," Daddy said. "He's gonna find out what happened to Mr. Taggert."

"I'm sure gonna try," Long said. "Terrible business, Mr. Ches. Ed Taggert was the manager of the whole operation. You can bet we'll catch the devil from headquarters." He shook his head. "We've called in the locals. Over yonder is Inspector Caesar from the Maracaibo cops. He seems like an all right fellow."

I followed Long's gaze across the big room to a well-dressed portly gentleman with well-coiffed white hair and a neatly trimmed mustache. He was talking to a pair of American workers, who spun their hats nervously in their hands.

"Do you have any clues yet?" I asked.

Long let out a sigh and shook his head. "Not many.

At first we thought it might be the Motilone Indians on the rampage again. Word is they're still angry about us driving them inland, but frankly, this just doesn't look like them. They like to attack in war parties, and they always use those god-awful long bows and six-foot arrows. A knife just isn't their style."

"I agree," Daddy said.

"I understand Ed Taggert had bad words with some of your boys out on the rig a few days ago." Long sat on the edge of the desk and motioned us to sit in the slatted folding chairs. "That's what I wanted to talk to you about this morning. That and take an official statement from Ricky about finding the body."

Daddy and I sat down.

"I'm sorry it had to be you, son, that found the body. I know that was a rough experience for you. How you holding up?"

"Okay. I guess."

"Fine. We'll talk in a minute."

"Anyway." Long turned back to Daddy. "I need to know everything that happened out on the rig that day. I understand Taggert fired a whole crew of natives, and my guess is one of them boys snuck back into the camp and paid the old man back."

Daddy gnawed on the stem of his pipe. "Well, now that would be one theory," he said. "Of course Taggert did have a way of getting under folks' skin."

"Mine included," Long tried to hide a weary smile. "But you know as well as I do, all those Venezuelan boys carry knives, and they all know how to use them. Seems like the way Mr. Taggert's throat got slit, well, that points at somebody who's handy with a blade."

"Well, I reckon it would."

"Plus we found some footprints out in the marshy area just past the pipe where young Ricky found the body."

Daddy nodded.

"Wonder if Mr. Taggert raised a holler?" I interrupted. "Seems like if somebody was chasing me with a knife, I'd yell my head off. See if I couldn't get some help."

Mr. Long grinned at me. "Well, that's good thinking son. We didn't see any signs of a chase or a struggle. Matter of fact, we're trying to get as many folks as we can in here today and ask them that very question. See if they saw or heard anything. Seems like most folks were out at the tennis courts watching the movie."

I shrugged. Surely somebody had heard something.

"I still think it's all gonna come down to one of them native boys that got fired on the job," Mr. Long said. "Inspector Caesar thinks he can locate all of 'em that went back across the lake to Maracaibo. He's gonna round them up and sweat 'em. I reckon we'll find the killer then."

"They seemed like good fellows to me," Daddy said. "Don't use your rubber hoses on 'em."

Long looked perplexed. "Whose side are you on, Mr. Ches?"

Daddy tapped his pipe in the palm of his hand.

"Side of justice, I reckon."

Long exhaled a breath through puffed cheeks. "I

see your point."

"Good." Daddy turned to me. "Ricky, go ahead and tell Mr. Long what you and your friend saw last night. Tell him just what you told your Mama and me." Daddy effectively cut off Mr. Long from any further discussion of the Venezuelans.

I told Mr. Long everything I remembered about finding the body and then Daddy took me over to the snack bar at the back of the Club. He bought me a chocolate ice-cream cone and then went back to talk to Mr. Long some more.

I ate my ice cream and wandered around the Club, hoping Hannah might show up. I couldn't wait to find her and talk about everything that had happened.

Only she never came.

Daddy finished his business with Mr. Long and we headed back to our house. The day was hot and muggy and my shirt was damp with sweat by the time we got home.

Mama fried some chicken for our noon meal and mashed some potatoes and made pan biscuits.

At the dinner table, Daddy told Mama all about what happened over at the Club. Then he said a strange thing. "Dixie, I reckon you'll be heading up to the Club this afternoon for bridge."

"I reckon so."

"Well, why don't you let me walk you up there. Then I'll come back later on in the evening and fetch you."

Mama pressed her lips into a thin line. "You're a mite scared, aren't you, Chester?"

"A mite."

"You're scared that whoever killed old man Taggert is lurking around out there somewhere, right?"

"Maybe."

"Well, yes, sir, Mr. Parker. I'd be obliged for you to escort me up to the Club this afternoon." Mama smiled and blushed and even got up from the table and did a little curtsy.

"Does this mean I can't go over to the baseball field?" I sopped up the last of the chicken gravy with the remains of my biscuit. I knew the answer before Daddy said anything.

"That's just what it means."

When Daddy used that tone, I knew there was no point in arguing.

So the rest of the afternoon I sat around in the living room, my leg draped over the arm of the chair, listening to the Andrews Sisters and Tommy Dorsey on Mama's phonograph, reading *Captain America*, *Batman,* and *Superman* comics and thinking about Hannah Oudt . . . and wondering who killed Mr. Taggert.

⟪ 10 ⟫

After supper that night, Daddy read his paper in the living room and Mama cleaned up the kitchen. All our newspapers came three or four days late from the states. Daddy said it was odd to always be reading about things that had happened days ago while knowing that other things had happened since and not know about them.

Mama finished up in the kitchen and headed into the living room to listen to some of her records. A few minutes later I went into the kitchen to get some water. I filled a glass at the sink, gulped it down, and when I turned around, Daddy was leaning against the doorframe watching me.

"You got a minute?" he asked.

"Sure."

Daddy sucked in air through his nose. It made a little whistling sound. "You and I been dancing around what happened over at the infirmary," he said. "What you said to me in the hallway 'fore the doctor sewed me up."

I nodded. "I shouldn't have said those things."

"No. Actually I think what you said was a good

idea. If you feel that strongly about something, you need to speak up. It's not good to keep all that stuff bottled up inside of you."

That made sense.

Daddy fiddled with his pipe, pushing the tobacco deep into the bowl. "I reckon I'm guilty of the same thing," he said. "I don't like to talk about things like that. Hurt feelings and such. I reckon I need to do more of it."

I had no idea what to say. Daddy had never said anything close to that in my whole life.

"You and I and Mama need to tell each other how we feel. Especially now with this god-awful murder. I've asked the two of you to make an enormous sacrifice. For me. For our country. These are tough times. Life's asking a lot of all of us. I want you to know that I'm proud of both of you. You've born the burden like real champions and I appreciate it."

You could have knocked me over with a feather. I leaned back against the sink.

"So you come tell me when you start feeling like you did over at the hospital. Don't keep it inside. We can always talk about it. You hear?"

I nodded. "Yessir."

"Good. That'll make it easier on everybody." Then Daddy smiled, turned around, and went back into the living room.

I drank another glass of water.

Around dusk, Uncle Harry showed up at the front door.

He was still in his work clothes from the derrick. His shirt had salty spots from the dried sweat that looked like badges and his heavy work pants were all dirty and greasy. He had dirt streaks on his cheeks. Mama made him go wash up out back. Then she dug out some cold chicken and mashed potatoes from the refrigerator and set a place for Uncle Harry at the little table in the kitchen. She and Daddy gathered round the table. Mama said I could have a Coca-Cola and sit on the stool by the counter and visit with Uncle Harry if I wanted.

I always wanted to listen to Uncle Harry.

"I hear you did yourself right proud last night," Uncle Harry said, wolfing down giant bites of chicken, washing them down with swigs from a bottle of Griesedieck Brothers beer. "Terrible thing for a boy your age to go through, but it sounds like you did all right. I'm proud of you."

"Thanks. It was really something. I'd never even seen a dead body," I said. "I was pretty scared."

"One thing's for sure. You'll grow up quick down here. It's tough territory. But you'll be fine. You come from good stock."

Mama chewed on her nails. She had been really cranky since we arrived at the camp and that night I got my first glimpse of how much she hated the wildness of the camp, the crudeness and the endless dirt. My mother hated the oil business.

"So what's the word around the Club?" Uncle Harry wiped his mouth on the back of his sleeve. "I've been out on the rig since before dawn."

Daddy sipped his own GB. "John Long's looking into things. He thinks it's an open and shut case. One of the native boys that Taggert fired out on the derrick the other day came back and took his revenge. Case closed."

"That sounds like John. But those boys? None of 'em seemed like the type to me."

"John's even let the locals in on the investigation. An Inspector Caesar from Maracaibo was over at the Club today."

Uncle Harry let out a snort. "A Venezuelan detective? The company people won't like that a bit."

"Well, maybe so," Daddy said. "But John is in over his head. So maybe this Caesar fellow can help out. He knows the natives. Maybe he can figure the thing out. Especially if the killer was one of his own."

"Ah, they may never figure out who killed old Taggert. If it was one of the native workers, he'll just fade into the crowded streets of Maracaibo or even head over to Caracas."

"You could be right," Daddy said.

Uncle Harry stared into his beer. "Well, one thing's for sure," he said. "With Taggert dead, I'm not gonna get that advance on my paycheck. Taggert was going to get back to me on that."

Daddy rolled his eyes. "Harry, Harry. Rich man's taste, workingman's budget."

Uncle Harry smiled. "The men on the rig today were pretty steamed," he said. He pushed his chair back, crossed his legs, and lit a smoke. "Some of 'em think it was the Motilones on the warpath. Not that I could blame those poor devils. They lived on the banks of the lake for years. Then the geologists discovered oil and the government and the company drove the Motilones out. Massacred a bunch of them. Women, children, everybody. Burned down their homes. Drove 'em into the wilderness. I'd be mad too."

"Not too different from back home," Daddy said.

"Right you are." Uncle Harry took a deep drag on his smoke. "I heard some ugly talk out on the rig today. Some of the fellows think we should round up the Indians and put 'em in prison camps."

"We tried that back home with the Cherokees. Didn't work too well. Just a lot of useless killing and too many widows and orphans."

"Amen, brother." Uncle Harry exhaled smoke out his nostrils.

"No wonder the folks down here hate us," Mama said. "We come into their country and take their oil and start talking about throwing folks into prison camps. I know we need the oil, but my gosh, how many lives is that black goo worth?"

"Now, Dixie. What the company's done isn't all bad," Daddy said. "I hear that before we came, Maracaibo was nothing but a swampland. Then Creole came in and built roads all around the lip of the lake, connecting the oil camps and the city, and lo and behold, Maracaibo is the second largest city in all of Venezuela. Now that's progress if you ask me."

"For us maybe," Uncle Harry said. "We've carted out everything the South Americans have—copper, sugar, tin, rubber, balsa wood. We just come down here, push the natives aside and take what we want."

"Dang it, Harry. You are so stubborn. We've paid for those goods and we're paying for the oil we're taking out. It's progress I tell you. At least some of it is and all progress comes with a price."

"A price? Look at the lake. It was beautiful once. Now it's coated with a film of oil."

"Well, I reckon you've pumped your share to make that happen, Mr. High and Mighty."

Daddy and Uncle Harry burst out laughing and clinked their beer bottles together. That was the way Uncle Harry and Daddy always were and I guess always had been. Daddy always wanted to look at all sides of an issue and try to see some good in everything and everybody. Uncle Harry always saw the bad, such as how the company exploited the workers and the natives and ruined everything it touched. But down deep, both of them loved working on the rigs.

I think Uncle Harry was a socialist or a communist or something. But whatever he was, he and my father loved each other and loved the good-natured banter that they shared over a few bottles of beer.

And Uncle Harry had a special place in my mama's heart. Sometimes it seemed like he was the only one who could drag a smile out of my mother. Especially since we moved to the oil camp. Some nights he'd come over and bring Mama some of the magazines she loved back home or maybe a bar of the special soap she liked.

How he got that stuff when no one else seemed able to, I'll never know. But it always made me happy to see Mama smile and, thanks to Uncle Harry, I'd feel like maybe everything would turn out all right.

Some nights Mama, Daddy, and Uncle Harry would listen to Glenn Miller on the phonograph, and Uncle Harry would turn to Daddy and say, "Would it be all right if I danced with your beautiful wife?" Daddy would nod and smile and go back to whatever he was puzzling over. Uncle Harry would whirl Mama around the room until the color returned to her face and maybe for a minute she'd be dressed in a beautiful gown, dancing in a fancy ballroom instead of a company house in a rough-and-tumble oil camp.

"Paper says the Germans are moving in on Leningrad," Daddy said.

"The Germans will have to kill every single man, woman, and child in the city," Uncle Harry said. "The Russians are tough. They'll never surrender."

"Knowing the Germans, that's just what they'll do," Mama added.

My mother's crack about the Germans made me squirm. "All the Germans aren't like that," I said.

My father and Uncle Harry turned around and looked at me like I was crazy.

"I bet a lot of them are nice folks." I just couldn't stop myself. "I bet a lot of them are not too different from the folks back in El Dorado."

"Well, that could be a good point, Son." Daddy fired up his pipe. "It's probably something we all need to keep in mind. But at the moment, all the Germans seem to be hypnotized by that Hitler fellow. Seems like they'll do anything that lunatic tells them to. And right now he's telling them to attack every peace-loving country in sight. France, Denmark, Russia. Wonder who'll be next?"

Mama busied herself cleaning up the kitchen. I decided not to say anything else about the Germans. I didn't want to tell anyone about Hannah, and I sure didn't want my father and Uncle Harry to think that I wasn't a one hundred percent loyal American.

Then they started talking about how important oil was gonna be for the war effort but that veered off into talking about some kind of new pumps out on the oil rigs and I decided to abandon ship.

"Y'all excuse me," I said, hopping off the stool. I'm going to my room." I didn't want to listen to any more talk about the murderous Germans and all the awful things they were doing.

I couldn't imagine Hannah doing any of those things. I knew the Germans were acting like bullies over in Europe and everybody thought they should be stopped, but somehow all that talk got mixed up with Hannah in my head. I just wanted to flop down on my bed and get lost in the adventures of Superman. So I left the kitchen.

I ran through *Superman* and *Batman* and *Captain Marvel* and after a while I felt sleepy. I went back into the living room, where Mama was reading a magazine and listening to the Andrews Sisters on the phonograph. She said Daddy and Uncle Harry were drinking beer out on the porch, catching up on old times.

I kissed Mama good night and went to bed.

The evening was hotter than hades, so I opened the window in my room wide and stripped down to my undershorts and just lay down on top of the sheets and sweated. After a while I rolled over and tried to find a dry, cool spot on the sheet, but then a couple of minutes later I'd have to roll over again and look for another one.

I could hear Uncle Harry and Daddy laughing out on the porch.

I drifted off to an uneasy sleep, but I woke up, feeling like I was in an oven dialed up to full blast. There was no air in my room. I got up, went over to the window, and lay down on the cool wood floor, trying to catch any little breeze that might drift by.

That didn't last long, because I could hear the mice under the house scurrying around. It sounded as if a whole army of rodents were massing right underneath my room. I sat up and rested my back against the wall beneath the window.

Uncle Harry's booming laugh drifted through the night. He had had a lot of beer. That's when he always got kinda loud. "It was history," he said. "You and me and Big Bill Haywood. Right there together fighting the good fight. Yessir, those were the times. We weren't afraid of nobody."

Daddy's voice was much lower. He said something about all that being a long time ago and now is now.

Then Uncle Harry said something that made my eyes pop wide open.

"I don't want to spread rumors, Ches, but it's a

fact. The Germans have a shortwave radio over in their compound, and I'm betting it's a powerhouse. They're talking to U-boats up in the straits just above the lake. Heck, we're sitting right on the edge of the Caribbean."

"Harry, how in the world do you know that?" Daddy said with a laugh.

When Uncle Harry answered, he wasn't laughing. "You know Oliver Hardin? The company geologist from Oklahoma? Lives over in the bachelor barracks."

"Sure."

"Oliver's a ham radio nut. He's got one up in his room. He's always fooling with the thing. Trying out different frequencies. Turning those little dials, listening to whatever he can find."

"So?"

"So he told me and Slim that he picked up some German talk on one of his weird frequencies. Oliver had a little German in high school and he swears the broadcast was coming from over in the German compound."

"Really?"

"You know the Nazi U-boats are out there. It just makes sense the Germans here are talking to them. We're sitting on one of the world's biggest supplies of oil. The Germans are gonna make a move. Sure as shootin'."

Daddy mumbled something I couldn't understand.

"We're in a dangerous situation here," Uncle Harry said. "This is war. Yessir, the Germans right here in this camp have got at least one big radio. And you want to know what I think?"

"I reckon you're gonna tell me anyway," Daddy said.

"I think Taggert found out about the radio. Maybe even found out where the Germans were hiding it. I think he went over to their compound, found the radio, and was heading back to tell John Long and his boys over in Security and one of the Germans killed him. Think about what I'm saying. Makes more sense than one of them native boys having the wherewithal to come all the way back over here from Maracaibo to slit the old man's throat. No sir. It had to be the Germans. They had to keep their radio a secret. That's who did it. I'd bet a month's wages I'm right."

"Let's don't be so quick to convict those folks 'fore all the evidence is in," Daddy said.

I pressed my back against the wall. Uncle Harry was talking about Hannah's father or one of her friends killing Mr. Taggert. And if the Germans really did have a radio hidden somewhere over in their compound and really were talking to the U-boats, the murder of Mr. Taggert suddenly made a lot of sense. But all I could see was Hannah's smile. All I could remember was how we stood on the banks of the creek and talked about how mean people were to each other. That and how much I still wanted to kiss her.

« 11 »

The inside of the Club was dark and cool and offered a welcome relief from the blazing sun and summer heat outside.

I paused in the doorway and let my eyes adjust to the dark. Two giant ceiling fans circulated the humid air and four oscillating fans in the corners helped bring down the temperature.

The Club was divided into two parts. The bar, off to the left of the entrance, where kids weren't supposed to go and the Great Room where everybody could go. The Great Room had sofas, ping-pong tables, a snack bar area, and clusters of chairs divided into separate conversation areas.

Mama was in the bar, playing bridge with three other ladies. I recognized the wives of some of the men who worked in the administration building. All four women studied their cards like their hand held the secrets of the universe.

I ignored the bar's ban on kids and crossed the room to the bridge table.

"I brought your reading glasses," I said as I approached the table.

My mother looked at me like I was crazy. That was not the kind of thing I normally did. "Oh. Why thank you, dear. That was sweet of you."

I handed the glasses case to my mother and smiled. She smelled like gin.

"Ricky, you know the ladies," Mama said, taking a long sip of her drink.

"Hi." I nodded at the other players. They all nodded back. All the ladies wore print dresses and bright red lipstick.

I caught my reflection in the mirror behind the bar. My hair was combed and my checked shirt and khaki shorts were neatly pressed. That was also not like me. Wrinkled T-shirts and dirty shorts were more my style.

"Everything okay?" Mom asked.

"Fine. I just wanted to bring you your glasses." That was a total lie. The glasses were an excuse to come to the Club and look for Hannah. Other than the baseball field, the Club was the only place I could think of where we might run into each other.

"You're a sweetheart," Mom said, giving me a look that said "shove off now."

Great by me.

I wandered back into the Great Room where I hit the jackpot.

Hannah Oudt sat at a table in the far back of the Great Room, talking to John Long and another man. The man's tie was pulled down, and he was sweating like he had just finished the hundred-yard dash. He had graying blond hair and sat ramrod straight. I assumed Mr. Long was talking to Hannah about the night we found Mr. Taggert's body. I didn't have a clue who the other man was.

An older woman sat on one of the sofas reading a thick book and a younger couple huddled together in conversation on another sofa. That was the whole crowd in the Great Room.

I bought a coke at the snack bar and wandered outside to the verandah. I didn't want Hannah to think I was looking for her. I wanted us to just run into each other.

I sat in one of the wicker chairs and sipped my coke. Eventually, Hannah would have to come out the front door so I was in no hurry. A couple of horses trotted by carrying a pair of oil-rig workers, their faces tanned nearly black by the sun. They waved as they passed the Club. I waved back.

After about twenty minutes, my patience was rewarded. The front door opened and Hannah wandered out onto the verandah. She stopped when she saw me. Then her face broke into a broad smile. I took that as a good sign.

"Ricky! Mein Gott. I was hoping I would run across you. I've been talking to Mr. Long of the security about . . . that night."

I jumped up and looked surprised. "Yeah. I was hoping to see you too. I've already talked to Mr. Long. Can you sit with me awhile?" I motioned to another wicker chair, where she sat without hesitating. "Could I get you a coke?" I indicated the empty bottle in my hand.

"Ja. Ja. If you please."

I went back to the snack bar and bought Hannah a coke. Everything was working out just like I hoped.

Back on the verandah, Hannah and I sat in wicker chairs and looked out at the dirt road in front of the Club, sipping our cokes. We watched a few people come and go from the company store down the street.

"Are you okay?" I said. "After . . . you know . . . what we found."

Hannah nodded. "I cried that night," she said. "But I am, how you say, all jake now."

"Right. Everything is jake."

Hannah wore a starched white blouse and a navy skirt. Her skin glowed a copper color from the sun. Her hair was clean and shiny.

"Had you ever seen a dead body before?" I asked.

"Ja. Once. My papa's mutter died of the old age when we were in Heidelberg. All the children gathered around the bed to tell her good-bye after she died. It was sad."

"I bet."

"My papa is in the Club now. He came with me to talk to Mr. Long. They are talking more now. Papa is concerned with several things in the camp. He never mentions them at home, but he welcomed the chance to talk to Mr. Long of the security. I will have to go with Papa when he finishes." I assumed Hannah's father was the blond man.

I hated to hear she'd have to leave. I wanted Hannah and I to spend the whole afternoon on the Club verandah together.

"Mr. Long thinks one of the native workers killed

Herr Taggert," Hannah said. "He asked if we saw such a person near the pipes that night. I told him nein."

I nodded my agreement. "I think he wants it to be one of the natives," I said. "It makes his job easier."

Hannah sipped her coke.

I wondered if she knew about the radio in the German compound. Uncle Harry was sure Mr. Taggert had found the radio the Germans used to talk to the U-boats and one of the Germans killed him. Would all the Germans know about the radio? I tried to think of a way to ask Hannah about the radio. There wasn't one.

"Mr. Long has no evidence the murderer was one of the natives," Hannah said. "Just his prejudice. Anyone could have killed Herr Taggert."

Anyone? Including one of her own people? I didn't want to think about it.

"I hope Herr Long will find the open mind." Hannah took another sip of her coke.

"Me too. I asked him if he thought Mr. Taggert called for help that night," I said. "Mr. Long said he didn't see any evidence of a struggle or that Mr. Taggert had been running away from the killer. Plus nobody seems to have heard anything. As I told him, I think I would have hollered my head off if some native had been chasing me with a knife." Or some crazed Nazi radio guy, I thought.

"But of course. Anyone would cry for help," Hannah said. "Perhaps Herr Taggert knew his assailant. He thought he was safe and saw no need to flee. Perhaps he was with a friend."

"Who turned out to not be a friend," I said. "Who

turned out to be a killer."

"Ja. My thought exactly."

Hannah was even prettier when she got worked up about something. Her eyes flashed with passion and her lips pushed out a little. It was really cute.

"You were so brave that night," Hannah said, locking onto my eyes. "You went right to see what had happened. Like a gentleman you kept me out of the way of harm. You are my knight in the shining armor."

Before I could put together a coherent response, the front door of the Club opened and Mr. Long and Dr. Oudt walked out onto the verandah. Dr. Oudt frowned when he saw me.

Hannah stood up. So did I. "Papa is not happy," Hannah said. "I will introduce you when the frame of his mind is better."

"Okay by me."

"We must talk again soon," Hannah said quickly as she started across the porch. "It is of much pleasure to see you."

"You too. Bye now." Our eyes lingered on each other.

And Hannah and her father were gone. Mr. Long nodded to me and disappeared back into the Club.

I sat on the verandah for a long time, watching the afternoon turn into evening.

I turned thirteen a couple of days later and my parents did the best they could under the circumstances to make my birthday feel like a special celebration but somehow nothing felt the same. I guess finding a dead body puts a damper on everything.

Mama baked a chocolate cake and fixed hamburgers, my favorite food in the whole world. Daddy brought home some ice cream from the Club and we shared a birthday meal at the kitchen table. Don't get me wrong. It was nice. But somehow it just missed.

If we had been back home in El Dorado, Daddy would have treated me and a couple of my pals to a double feature at the Rialto and then Mama would have served a big dinner on the picnic table in the backyard for me and my friends and the guys would have given me some comic books or a baseball or something fun. Because of the tough economic times, Mama and Daddy usually stuck to more practical gifts like a new shirt or a jacket.

Then the guys would have stayed over and we would have spent the night out on the sleeping porch, talking baseball and telling stories about some of the girls in our class and cutting farts and laughing till the sun came up.

But in Venezuela everything was different. I didn't know any kids except the fellows at the baseball field and so the party was just me and Mama and Daddy. We didn't cut any farts or even laugh much. But it was nice. They gave me a pair of khaki pants. Mama said I really needed them for the new school year that was about to start.

Before I blew out the candles on the cake, Uncle Harry showed up and the party got more lively. He walked in with his hand behind his back. He wished me a happy birthday, brought his hand out in front of him, and handed me a brand new catcher's mitt.

I couldn't believe it. Where on earth did Uncle Harry find a new catcher's mitt in an oil camp in the middle of Venezuela? But that was the way Uncle Harry was—he made the impossible possible. And it was a great mitt, stiff with that wonderful fresh leather smell. I loved it.

After that Mama and Daddy and Uncle Harry sang "Happy Birthday" to me while I blew out the candles on the cake. Uncle Harry couldn't carry a tune in a bucket, but he sang with a lot of fervor and kinda drowned out everybody else. We all laughed and I guess my birthday party was turning out to be fun after all.

But it got better.

After dinner Mama cleaned up the kitchen while Daddy and Uncle Harry took their coffee into the living room and fell into a discussion about oil-rig machinery.

The night was clear and warm and I wandered out into the backyard to look at the stars and think about what it meant to finally be in my teens. Only I never got around to that.

As I walked down the back stairs, I stumbled over a little wicker basket that was sitting on the bottom step. I picked up the basket and sat down on the stairs. A full moon lit up the backyard with a soft golden glow.

The top of the basket was covered with a red-and-white checked cloth. I peeled back the cloth and the most wonderful smell leaped up at me. Strudel. Two strudels. One with apples and one with cherries. Plus a small folded note.

I opened the note and read the message that was printed in neat block letters.

> *Happy Birthday, Ricky.*
>
> *Your new friend, Hannah*

Hannah! It was a birthday gift from Hannah Oudt. My heart started thumping like a bass drum. Hannah. Wow.

Only how did the basket get on our back stairs? I had mentioned my birthday to Hannah at the baseball field, but I never expected anything as great as a present.

Hannah Oudt had brought me a present. Talk about the greatest thing since sliced bread. Hannah Oudt had been thinking about me. Just like I had been thinking about her.

This birthday had late night fart jokes beat by a mile.

« 12 »

School started later that week and my good mood from Hannah's gift went steadily downhill. The more I thought about it, Uncle Harry's explanation of who killed Mr. Taggert made all the sense in the world to me. There was a war raging all over Europe and the Creole Camp was smack-dab in the middle of one of the richest oil-producing areas on the whole planet. It all added up. The Germans in the camp had a big radio and were talking to a U-boat somewhere in the Caribbean, planning God knows what. Mr. Taggert found the radio and the Germans killed him. Uncle Harry was a smart guy.

But where did that leave me? Out in the cold with a major league crush on Hannah Oudt, that's where. Only I didn't even know when I could see her again. I didn't have the nerve to just walk right into the German compound. No telling what would happen to me if I did that. But I really, really wanted to see her in the worst way and Saturday's baseball game looked like my best bet. If my father would let me go.

But in the meantime I had to get the eighth grade off and running. Not as easy as it sounds.

The Creole Camp school was weird. All the eighth graders, about a dozen of us, started the day in Mrs. Sullards' homeroom, and then moved around all together to our other classes during the day.

There were also about a dozen seventh graders, and they did the same thing, except they started the day in Mr. Kent's room. There were four classrooms and four teachers in our wing of the school. The other wing of the school was full of little kids and none of us ever went over there.

Mrs. Sullards taught math and science. She was young and pretty with short dark hair and a great smile. She was from Beaumont, Texas and was married to one of the geologists that worked over in the administration building. She always had something nice to say to everybody.

Mr. Kent acted like a girl, waving his hands around and wiggling his hips when he walked. He taught English and made us memorize a lot of poetry.

Across the hall, Mr. Shaver taught history. He was short and cross-eyed, but he was really funny and really knew a lot about history. He was probably older than Daddy, and the rumor around school was that he had once been a professor at some college in Kansas but got fired.

The last room belonged to Senorita O'Connell, who was from some little town in Iowa or Indiana and taught Spanish. It made a lot of sense to learn Spanish, seeing as we were living in a Spanish-speaking country. It made no sense to be in a classroom with Senorita O'Connell. Her mousy brown hair always stuck out in different directions and she cried a lot. Right in the middle of class. Her nose was always red.

My guess was the senorita came to Venezuela looking for adventure and romance. What she got was a room full of smart-ass junior high kids, who were lonesome for home back in the states and were left on their own a lot because their daddies worked off on the rigs and their mamas were tied to the bridge tables over in the Club. Plus I suspect she lied about her fluency in Spanish.

The first couple of days, Senorita O'Connell tried to teach us about Venezuela. She read everything out of a book in a dull monotone, and she might as well have been talking about some place on Mars. "The most important region is the coastal strip—humid lowlands and the bordering foothills which stretch from Lake Maracaibo to the Orinoco delta in the east."

No wonder everyone hates junior high school.

"Venezuela. Little Venice was the name given to the region of Lake Maracaibo by explorers who sailed in from the sea and saw native huts on stilts in the shallow, brackish waters."

Sonny Cole tore off a piece of paper from his notebook, wadded it up, put the paper in his mouth, chewed it thoughtful, took it out, rolled it in his hand, and then hit this guy name Asa square in the back of the head with the paper wad. Everyone in the class giggled.

Senorita O'Connell never looked up. "Maracaibo was founded in 1567 in large part because of the early slave trade in Indians." Asa threw a pencil at Sonny. Giggles escalated to laughs.

The Senorita plowed on. "Through the efforts of the three dominant oil companies, Shell, Gulf, and Standard, by 1941 Venezuela is now the world's first exporter of petroleum and the world's second producer after the United States. The Creole Petroleum Company processes over half of Venezuela's petroleum."

Sonny shot Asa the bird. That resulted in an avalanche of giggles from everybody. Asa gave Sonny the double bird. The giggles escalated.

"And Venezuela has its own heroes." The Senorita looked out the window like she expected some dashing South American Casanova to ride up on a white stallion and save her. "Like Simon Bolivar, a wealthy creole who traveled in Europe and read Voltaire. He was handsome and brilliant."

Senorita O'Connell scanned the horizon again. "And he led over 2,000 soldiers on a daring march through the Andes to stage a surprise attack on the Spanish oppressors. After that he—"

Sonny stuck his finger in his mouth and then leaned forward and put his wet finger in Robby Snedden's ear. The class roared.

Senorita O'Connell burst into tears.

The Senorita wasn't the only one having a tough time at the Creole company school. Right off the bat I figured out that all the kids in my grade fell into two groups. Sonny and Asa and Billy Barton and a couple of other guys that played baseball were one group. They spent all the time between classes together and ate lunch together outside under the pear trees that formed a little grove above the baseball field. They were always joking around and punching each other on the shoulder and doing guy stuff.

The other group consisted of dumpy Robby Snedden, skinny, creepy Joel England, who picked his nose all the time, Lamar Johnson, who breathed through his mouth and didn't even seem to know he was in Venezuela, and the three girls in the class—Bess and Tess, the twins, and Sylvia Morrison, who was a head taller than anyone else in the eighth grade.

Because we had played baseball earlier, I figured I'd hang around with Sonny and those guys. Boy, was I wrong.

The first day, I took my lunch over to the pear tree. "Hey. Did you guys see where the Cardinals took over second in the National League? My dad brought home a stack of papers yesterday. Walker Cooper's on a hot streak."

Sonny Cole looked up from his half-eaten sandwich. "I don't follow baseball back home. Too much trouble." The tone of his voice said 'get lost.'

But like Senorita O'Connell, I plowed on. "We gonna have a game again this Saturday? I mean, school starting doesn't change anything, does it?"

Asa blew air out of the side of his mouth. "We ain't got enough players," he said. "My old man says the company ain't gonna let any more natives over in our camp. Not even to play ball. He says all the Venezuelans are stupid and lazy anyway."

Suddenly I would rather have eaten lunch in a pit

of cottonmouth water moccasins than with Asa and the rest of those idiots.

Sonny looked up from his sandwich "I reckon you think you're the cat's pajamas these days. Finding old man Taggert's body and all."

"Not really. I mean it was kinda gross if you want to know the truth."

"And I don't think the Germans are gonna come play baseball anymore either," Billy Barton said, talking with his mouth full of pasty tuna. "Something is going on with them. Something happened that nobody will talk about."

The radio, I thought. Other people know about the German's hidden radio.

"My Mama said the Huns better keep their butts way over on their side of the camp if they know what's good for them. Those two little German creeps weren't good ball players anyway." Billy's face was a giant smirk. "So see, we don't have enough players. Baseball's over for the year." His tone clearly told me to take a hike.

So I did.

I walked away in a fog. No more baseball games on Saturday. That meant no Hannah. My worst nightmare.

Snedden, England, and the girls were eating under the little kid's jungle gym on the far side of the building. They all pushed their heads close together and started giggling when I walked by them, so I ate my paper bag lunch all by myself in the shade of the school building on the side by the road.

The next day I brought some comics and read them while I ate my lunch.

Eating lunch by myself wasn't as bad as it sounds. I don't mind being by myself. Actually I kinda like being by myself. I can read comics and think about baseball and stuff. No people to bug me. It's not the worst thing in the world. Once you get used to it.

Why didn't the other kids take to me? Probably lots of reasons. As far as Sonny Cole was concerned, I think I embarrassed him that day at the baseball field when me and Romulo went after the tarantulas and he turned chicken. The other guys, Asa and Billy Barton, were scared that day as well and they knew it. And I knew it. We're all scared sometime, but we don't want anyone else to know it.

But that day everybody knew those guys were scared and two outsiders, me and Romulo, weren't scared and we showed Sonny and the other guys up.

Nobody wants to be friends with a guy who shows them up.

Snedden and those kids? I think they were just comfortable with their little group, and like most folks, were suspicious of strangers. They weren't bad kids. They just didn't want anything to change.

After a week of school nothing had changed.

Then things got worse.

Over in Europe, the Nazis killed thousands of Russians and bombed London and God knows what. In China, the Japanese were killing and bombing and blowing up cities and committing horrible crimes against the Chinese people.

And in the Creole Camp, everybody was tense about Mr. Taggert's murder. Some people thought the killer was still on the loose, hiding in the pipes or out in the jungle, waiting to attack someone else and cut their throat.

Even my school day got off to a bad start. Early in the morning, just before class started, Joel England, Robby Snedden, and the twins were horsing around on this merry-go-round over on the little kids playground. The boys were pushing the girls faster and faster in a circle, running over the worn out earth beneath the merry-go-round, and Tess and Bess were squealing in the way that girls squeal that says keep pushing, make us go faster.

But somehow Snedden's feet got tangled up with England's and Snedden lost his balance and pitched forward and one of the merry-go-round handles bonked him square in the forehead and split open an ugly cut right across the middle of his head.

Blood gushed over his eye and dripped down on his shirt and poor Snedden cried, which I knew he'd be sorry about later. But the poor guy couldn't help it. Tess, or maybe it was Bess, shrieked and cried too.

The other twin sprinted into the school building and Mrs. Sullards came running. She was calm and seemed to know just what to do. She sent England in to fetch the first aid kit and the rest of us inside with instructions to do all the math problems on pages 22 and 23.

Then she took the sniveling Snedden over to the infirmary. Mr. Kent was giving some kind of test in his class, and he prissed in and out of our class to make sure we didn't burn down the building while Mrs. Sullards took care of Robby.

Our homeroom teacher came back to school about noon in a dark mood. She sat on the edge of the desk and told us that Robby was okay, but the infirmary didn't have any iodine or antibiotic cream. She said she was worried that poor Robby might get an infection.

Things settled down after lunch. At least for a while.

We trooped into Mr. Shaver's classroom for our afternoon history lesson. Mr. Shaver was closely following the war in Europe and had a big map with red pins in it to show the areas where the Germans had moved in and taken over.

He talked a lot about how awful things were over there and how powerful the German panzer divisions were and how the Nazi troops killed everyone or enslaved everyone. He talked a lot about innocent people dying for the blood and land lust of the Nazi monster.

Tall Sylvia asked Mr. Shaver if he thought the Germans would one day attack the United States. She especially wanted to know if the Nazis might attack her home in Alabama, which Sylvia, for some reason, thought was very close to Germany.

Mr. Shaver pressed his lips together. "That's the most important question anyone can ask these days," he said. "Thank you, Sylvia. What do you all think?"

"If they attack us, we'll kick their butts all the way back to Berlin," Billy Barton blurted out.

"Will we, Billy? Last I heard we had a small army and a lot of outdated equipment," Mr. Shaver said. "Could America defeat the highly trained panzer divisions? The same ones that have virtually conquered Europe?"

Billy slumped down in his seat.

"We whipped 'em in the last war," Asa piped up. "The Great War. That's what you said last term."

"And we did," Mr. Shaver said quietly. "But this is a new war. I'm not sure we're ready this time."

I raised my hand. "What about Lend Lease? Won't that help the Allies win the war?" Ever since I'd overhead Daddy and Uncle Harry talking about the secret radio I'd been reading Daddy's newspapers all about the war.

"Good point, Ricky. But shouldn't we send them men and guns as well as supplies? Isn't it our job to protect democracy and freedom wherever it's challenged anywhere in the world?"

I should have quit while I was ahead. The war in Europe was about "the Germans" not about Hannah. Wars are never about people you know and like. People you care about. Wars are only about the evil people that you don't know, doing evil things that you must stop. Right?

But all I could think about was how awful it would be for my country to be at war with Hannah's country. How horrible it would be for my people to be killing her people. And vice versa.

"Maybe this war is none of our business," I said. "Maybe the Europeans can settle it themselves. Maybe if we sent over enough trucks, tanks, and guns and even oil, maybe we won't have to get involved." It was the best I could do.

Behind me somebody made a clucking noise like a chicken.

Mr. Shavers held up his hand, but somebody else started clucking. And then someone else picked up the sound. And someone else. The whole room suddenly sounded like the henhouse back home in El Dorado.

And right then and there I knew I was going to eat every lunch all by myself for the rest of the year.

《 13 》

"You can't just sit around the house and mope forever." Mama sat on the edge of my bed. "I know things are not going well over at the school, and I'm sorry, Ricky. I really am. Moving down here has been hard on all of us."

It was early Saturday afternoon and I hadn't gotten out of bed yet. I had no reason to get out of bed. The Saturday afternoon baseball games had gone down the toilet, the kids at school thought I was a yellow belly, Hannah was hiding out in the German compound, and I had read every comic book I owned at least ten times.

Mama wanted to cheer me up, but she wasn't doing a very good job. It's hard to cheer someone up when you're mostly in the dumps yourself. Recently, that was where Mama had been spending her days.

My mother had always been beautiful. Back in El Dorado, when she would come down to the school, I was always proud of her. Daddy felt the same way. When Mama got dressed up to go somewhere, Daddy's eyes would shine just looking at her.

Yes, Mama was definitely movie star beautiful until we moved to the oil camp. After we got to the

Creole Camp, Mama quit painting her fingernails and fussing with her beautiful hair, making it all bouncy and picture perfect. Her nails and makeup, the luster of her hair all faded the longer we were away from our home in Arkansas.

But she tried her best to chase away my blues. "Tell you what," she said. "You get up and do a few chores, maybe go out and play some, practice your grounders, and I'll fix hamburgers for supper tonight. I hear the company store got in some fresh meat yesterday. I'll stop by after bridge and get some. I'll fry up some potatoes. How does that sound?"

Actually, hamburgers and all the trimmings sounded pretty good.

"Okay. It's a deal then. Your father's out on the rig all day today, and I'm heading over to the Club. There's a box of cornflakes and some powdered milk on the kitchen table. Get up, sweetie. This isn't normal for a boy your age. You need to be up and about. Chop-chop now."

I was tempted to tell Mama about Hannah. About how I felt about her. About how every time I thought about Hannah this weird energy went surging through me. About how thinking about Hannah made a lot of bad stuff seem better.

But I didn't tell Mama.

All my life I'd told my parents everything. Well, okay, I didn't tell them about seeing Elmer's sister naked. But I always told them other stuff. All the important stuff. But Hannah was too special. I didn't want to share my feelings about her with anyone. Just to say it out loud might make it seem less special.

So I kept my mouth shut.

After Mama left for her bridge game, I stayed in bed for a while longer, then got up, put on a pair of shorts and the same blue shirt I had worn to school the day before, and laced up my Keds. I went into the kitchen and had two bowls of cornflakes and a couple of pieces of cold bacon I found wrapped up in wax paper in the refrigerator.

The food made me feel a little better, and I decided to rejoin the human race, at least for a while. I found Daddy's newspaper in the living room. It was only three days old. The Cardinals had lost to the Dodgers, and it looked like the Red Birds weren't going to make the World Series after all. Lon Warneke, the Arkansas guy, pitched well but got hurt in the eighth and Brooklyn scored three runs and won, 3–2.

The war news was awful. The Germans were advancing on Leningrad. In France, the Nazis had executed fifteen French Jews for spying. In China, the Japanese had taken a couple of cities I couldn't pronounce and killed several hundred inhabitants.

I thought about going back to bed.

Instead, I washed the dishes, put them away, and then went out and mowed the tiny front lawn. Daddy insisted I do that every Saturday. Then I made some lemonade and sat around in the living room, drinking the lemonade and rereading a couple of *Captain Marvel* comics.

Bored restlessness finally drove me out of the house, but not without a plan. Or at least kind of a plan.

I hiked past the bachelor's barracks and turned down the trail. When I looked back up at the barracks, I saw Uncle Harry sitting at a picnic table behind the building, talking to the doctor from the infirmary. They were smoking and deep in conversation, so I decided not to circle by and say hello. Besides, I was scared if I stopped, I'd lose my nerve and not follow through with my plan.

I went on down the path and then took the back road by the giant pipes. Nothing had happened for several weeks, and I didn't think anyone thought whoever killed Mr. Taggert was still lurking around the camp. Everything had pretty much returned to normal.

And why not? Everyone was probably safe, especially if Uncle Harry was right about the radio in the German compound.

I skipped rocks across the creek, which wasn't too hard since the water level was low. I horsed around in the pipes for a while. The day was muggy like most days on the shores of Lake Maracaibo and my shirt and my hair got damp.

Every time I thought about my plan, my hands got clammy and my stomach started hurting. Maybe the bacon had been bad or I had the flu and should go home. I was kidding myself. I felt fine.

Finally, with a deep breath and a loud exhale and a last rock across the creek, I launched a direct charge on the German compound.

I thought there might be heavy gates with armed guards

at the entrance, but there was none of that stuff. I just walked in. Just like that. There were more big trees than we had in the American compound. I figured that was because the Germans lived so close to the creek. The first building was a one-story social hall at the end of a short gravel driveway. This was the place Hannah had told me about where the Germans like to gather and drink German beer and sing German songs. And maybe salute the swastika and "Heil Hitler" each other all evening. Hannah told me the Germans never felt comfortable at the Club everyone else used. They like to be with their own kind.

A nice size swimming pool sat in back of the social hall. The pool was bigger than the municipal pool back in El Dorado and even had marked lanes for lap swimming and a bathhouse on the far side. A couple of women in bathing suits and caps were standing in the shallow end of the pool, splashing around with a pair of little kids. One of the women shot me a dirty look as I looped around the driveway.

The houses in the German compound weren't any bigger than the ones over on our side of the camp, but they seemed bigger. The lawns were all deep green and immaculately trimmed. Every house had both flowerbeds and flower boxes crammed full of colorful flowers. Even the cracks in the concrete in the driveways had been patched. Someone had taken a lot of time to rake the dirt road and smooth out the surface.

After walking about a block or so, I spotted a woman on her hands and knees trimming the edges of her lawn with a pair of heavy clippers. "Excuse me," I said, standing behind her in the road.

The woman turned around and looked at me like I was a creature from outer space. "Ja?"

"Hi." I planted a big smile on my face. "I'm looking for Hannah Oudt. I was wondering if you could direct me to her house."

"Hannah? Oudt? Oh, ja, ja. Herr Professor Oudt. Ja. Walk to end of der block." She pointed with the clippers. "Turn to the left. Three, four houses down. The Oudts. Look for the blue shutters. Only blue shutters on the street. Ja?"

"Fine. Thank you. Your yard is lovely."

The woman smiled a little. "Danke." She nodded her head in that knowing, motherly way. "Hannah. Ja." Her head bobbed and her smile grew wider.

I don't know what I expected, but the German woman was just, well . . . a woman out trimming her walkway on a sunny Saturday afternoon. Maybe I thought she'd at least be wearing a pistol on her hip or have a machine gun close by. After all, it was wartime for them.

Anyway, I strolled on down the street, following the woman's directions. Hannah had told me that most of the German workers had left the camp and gone home, yet every one of the houses remained well cared for, even though it was obvious no one lived in them. I tried looking in some of the front windows from my vantage point in the street and saw the familiar white sheets that covered the furniture in company housing.

My steps involuntarily slowed the closer I got to Hannah's house. I wanted to get there, but apparently not too quickly.

And then . . . there it was, the white house with blue shutters at the end of the block. Between the houses I could see the creek over a tall wooden fence. A pair of stout pine trees guarded the front of the house.

I had been hoping and praying and praying and hoping that Hannah would somehow be in the front yard. You know, maybe sitting around in a porch swing or sitting on the front steps or something. But she was nowhere in sight.

I stood in the road for a while and then decided that loitering in the street might look suspicious, so I marched up to the front porch and knocked on the door.

Hannah opened the door, and the smile that instantly blossomed across her face let me know that my plan had worked. "Ricky. Hallo." She had on a dress with rust-colored flowers on a cream background. Her hair was pinned up. She smelled like strawberry soap.

"Hi. I thought I'd, uh, stop by and say hi. See how you were doing. Uh, how are you doing?"

"I am fine. Please, please come in." Her hand fluffed her hair.

I followed her into the house. The living room was neat and sparsely furnished. A card table in the corner was covered with big books and notebooks. "My homework," Hannah said. "Papa says I must master the calculus before I can go forward with my mathematical studies."

I didn't even know what calculus was. Mrs. Sullards had started us on algebra and that was hard enough.

"Keeping you busy, huh?"

Hannah nodded. "Ja. For the most part. Papa is a hard taskmaster."

I nodded. "I hadn't seen you since that day over at the Club, and I, uh, just wanted to say hi."

"It was nice visit," Hannah said. "I wanted that we have more time together."

"Me too."

"Thank you for coming. Please come and meet Werner and meine Mutter."

I shrugged. "Sure."

We passed through the kitchen and went out onto a screened-in porch in the rear of the house.

Little Hans was sleeping in a basket on the floor, his thumb planted snugly in his mouth.

A man who was somewhere in his middle twenties and an older woman with her hair in a tight bun sat in a pair of wicker chairs at one end of the porch. They both stood as Hannah and I entered the room.

"Mutter, das is Ricky, the boy that was with me the night the supervisor died. He has come to pay his respects. Ricky this is meine Mutter."

Mrs. Oudt extended her hand. "Welcome, young man. Hannah speaks highly of you."

We shook hands. "Nice to meet you," I said.

"Hannah speaks of you often," the young man said without a smile.

"My older brother, Werner," Hannah said. "Werner works with the rig workers out at the land camp. The crews work four fourteen-hour days in the field and then come back here for a few days before going back. He got home yesterday." She gave her brother a playful squeeze on the arm.

Werner and I shook hands. "It is a pleasure to make your acquaintance." The guy sounded like he was practicing his English. He stood ramrod straight like a soldier standing at attention. He had neatly trimmed brown hair and steel blue eyes that gave me the once-over. His nose and chin were pointy and his face had the dark tan of someone who worked outside a lot.

It could have been an awkward moment but it wasn't. Werner and Mrs. Oudt invited me to sit down in another wicker chair and made every effort to make me feel comfortable. Mrs. Oudt disappeared into the house for a few minutes and then returned with a tray filled with teacups and tiny cakes.

I didn't like tea, but I piled in sugar and cream and the tea wasn't so bad. The little cakes tasted terrific.

Nobody mentioned the war. They asked me what I was studying over at the school, and we talked about the derricks and how their production had increased since Daddy took over as drilling supervisor.

Werner said Herr Professor Oudt was working at the administration building, plotting possible sights for new land rigs. They told some family stories that made Hannah's father sound like the original absentminded professor. Apparently he was always forgetting his glasses were perched on the top of his head or wearing his heavy coat out in the summer sun because he had forgotten the season had changed.

"Thank you so very much for saving young Hans

from the terrible spiders," Mrs. Oudt said. "Hannah told us all about your heroics. And of course we are in your debt for helping Hannah the night of Herr Taggert's untimely death. You are clearly a young American gentleman."

I shrugged and felt my cheeks getting red.

"What a terrible thing that befell Herr Taggert," Werner said. "He was doing such an outstanding job in reorganizing the work on the derricks. Is there news on who committed such a foul deed?"

"I don't think anybody knows much right now," I said. "I know the company's head of security is working on the case and there's a detective from Maracaibo working on it. That's about all I know."

Werner nodded. "In the American movies they always bring the guilty party to justice. I am sure this will also be the case here. American justice will prevail. Ja?"

"Yeah, I guess."

The conversation ran out of gas for a minute. Then Hannah came to the rescue. "Have you seen the Angel Falls?"

I felt a smile creep across my face. Mrs. Sullards thought Angel Falls was the Eighth Wonder of the World. "No," I laughed. "But one of my teachers at school told us it's even better than the pyramids of Egypt."

"Werner has seen it from an aeroplane."

"Ja." Werner nodded. "A most breathtaking sight."

"Mrs. Sullards said it's named after a fellow named Jimmy Angel," I said. "She said Angel was a test pilot from Kansas. She told our class Angel was doing geological explorations and he'd heard all these stories about this mountain. Back in '34 he found the mountain, and came back and reported to the Venezuelans that they had the tallest waterfall in the whole world."

"Ja," Werner said. "I hear the same story."

Hannah smiled at me. "Maybe someday soon you and I could see the Angel Falls together," she said. "I get so tired of the camp. And to see something like that with . . . my new friend would be wonderful. Ja?"

Talk about a great idea. Seeing Angel Falls with Hannah. Just she and I and this big, beautiful waterfall. Could anything be more wonderful than that?

"Count me in," I said, trying not to look too pleased. "You and me and Angel Falls."

Hannah looked deep into my eyes. I looked back. The rest of the world faded deep into the background.

Werner frowned, but I ignored him.

We chatted politely for a while longer and then Werner excused himself to go up to the social hall and have a swim. Mrs. Oudt said she had to slip next door for a few minutes and get a recipe from her neighbor.

Hannah and I sat on the porch and looked out at the bubbling creek behind the house.

"Since we found Herr Taggert's body, life has become more difficult for the Germans in the camp," Hannah said quietly.

"What d'you mean?"

"The Americans do not believe in the Fatherland. They prefer the arrogance of the English. Or even the bohemianism of the French. They even prefer the red bolshevism of the Russians. Wherever we go now in the camp, the Americans look at us like vermin. It is better that we stay in the compound. Our fathers and brothers do their work and return. It is not much better than prison."

I nodded. "A lot of folks think the U.S. will go to war with Germany soon."

Hannah sighed. "It makes me sad. So much war. So much killing. And more to come. I wish I had met you in another time. Another place, perhaps. Things might be different."

I was just happy to be there with Hannah at that moment in that place. That was all I could think about.

"We should have more tea," Hannah said. "I know you would like another cake. Come help me fix the tea."

We went into the kitchen, which was as small as a ship's galley and cleaner than an operating room. Hannah fussed around with the tea stuff, put the kettle on the stove, and found some more little cakes and placed them on the tray. She asked me to look in the pantry for some more sugar.

The pantry was large enough to stand in. It was crammed full of canned goods, all arranged in neat rows. Hannah stepped into the pantry behind me.

And that's when it happened.

I turned around and we just looked at each other for a minute. Then I tilted my head and she tilted her head and I kissed her. Right on the mouth. Lips on lips.

Time seemed to stop as Hannah put her arms

around me, and I put my arms around her and held her tight. We kissed again. Then we looked into each other's eyes and kissed again.

Then the stupid teakettle went off and we heard Mrs. Oudt coming in the back door. The magic moment vanished. Hannah and I jumped apart, and Hannah went back into the kitchen to finish making the tea. I just stood there and tried to reign in my breathing and hold on to the moment as long as I could.

« 14 »

After The Kiss, Mrs. Oudt joined us for more tea. I could feel my face burning the whole time. I was relieved when Hannah's mom finally suggested that Hannah and I go up to the social hall and join Werner and some of his friends for a swim.

Hannah dug out an old bathing suit of Werner's and told me I could change at the bathhouse. She put on her own suit at the house, and let me tell you, Hannah in her white bathing suit took my breath away. She draped a white beach towel over her shoulders and slipped into a pair of slippers.

We walked and skipped and ambled up to the swimming pool at the social hall, stealing little glances at each other, bumping into each other whenever we could, just for the thrill of touching.

When we got to the pool, Werner was standing in the shallow end, talking to a fellow about his age and a girl who looked a little younger. Both of them were sitting on the edge of the pool with their legs dangling in the water. Werner smiled and waved when he saw us.

The bathhouse smelled strongly of mildew and chlorine. The men's locker room had wooden lockers where I hung my pants and shirt on nails when I changed into Werner's old bathing suit. In the back of the bathhouse, a narrow curved metal staircase led to the upstairs.

A chunky bald man sat on a wooden folding chair next to the staircase. He wore a rumpled blue suit and a maroon tie with the knot pulled down. He was reading a newspaper through half-closed eyelids.

I shrugged and checked my hair in the tiny mirror on the wall by the lockers. My hair? I had never given a hoot how my hair looked. Now my stupid hair seemed like the most important thing in the world.

Out in the pool, Hannah introduced me to Fritz and his sister Gertie, the couple Werner had been talking to. They seemed nice. Fritz worked on the inland rigs with Werner.

"Only until next month," Fritz said in a clipped accent. "Then I shall return to the Fatherland to go into the army."

I didn't say anything.

"I shall be doing the same in the spring," Werner said, gently splashing water up on Gertie, who he obviously wanted to impress.

I still didn't say anything.

"But even in working here, we have been able to serve the Fatherland," Fritz said. "When the war ends, we will need strong men who can draw the oil from the land. We will control much land with oil. In the Caucasus, and certainly in the Arab world. It will take oil to run the cars and trucks and jeeps and aeroplanes. It will take oil to rule the world. It will take oil for the

Fatherland to fulfill its destiny."

I figured it already took oil to bomb all those innocent people in England and France. It took oil to drive the German army deep into Russia where they measured the deaths in hundreds of thousands. This was more than I could take. I opened my mouth.

Hannah must have figured out a disaster was on the way, so she splashed water in my face with her palm. "Come, Ricky. The afternoon is far too hot to stand around and talk of politics and war. While we are young, we should play."

I was grateful Hannah had cut me off. Werner and Fritz were big and tough looking, and I was a little scared of them. Not that I would have backed down, but still . . .

Fritz stuck out his jaw and barked something at me in German.

"What'd he say?" I turned to Hannah.

Hannah's lips were set in a thin line. "Is of no mind. This is our day and we shall enjoy it. Come." She took my hand and we pushed our way through the water, toward the center of the swimming pool, away from Fritz and the others.

"So come on, what'd he say?" I leaned in close to Hannah and whispered.

Hannah shook her head no.

"Come on," I said. "Let me in on what's going on."

We moved toward the end of the pool. "Hannah. What did he say?"

Hannah let out a deep sigh. "I will only tell you so you will be careful. Fritz is a dangerous young man. He is, as you Americans say, a hothead. He loves the Fatherland and he hates Americans. He thinks you want to prevent the Germans from achieving their destiny."

"Could be," I said, irritated with the whole thing.

"He says you should stay away from our compound. Unless you want to end up in the pipe like Herr Taggert."

"Where does he get off . . ."

Hannah sighed again. "And . . ."

"And what?"

Hannah looked over my shoulder at Fritz and the others. She lowered her voice. "And he is jealous."

"Jealous?"

"Ya. Of you and me. He is, how do you say it, sweet on me. Even though I think he is a clod."

"Good to know," I said.

Hannah blushed and looked uncomfortable.

"Okay," I said. "Enough of this. Like you said, let's enjoy our day."

Hannah grinned and nodded.

We swam out into the deep end of the pool and frog kicked and splashed around and then did some dives off the low board. I was a pretty good diver, having spent a lot of hot summer afternoons back in Arkansas diving off the high bank into the deep pools of Bodcau Creek.

Hannah was no slug on the diving board herself. She approached the edge of the board with practiced precision, bounced gracefully off the end, and sprung into the air with the sleekness of an eagle. She hardly made a ripple when she hit the water.

The two German boys who played baseball with us over at the school field showed up and another girl came. I got the impression that the pool was the place to hang out on a steamy Saturday afternoon if you were a young German in the Creole compound. They all eyed me with a strange look, but nobody said anything. A couple of young mothers and their small children splashed around in the shallow end of the pool.

Somebody came up with a partly deflated soccer ball, and we all fell into an impromptu, disorganized game of water polo. We didn't even have any goals. All you had to do was hit a wooden chair that Werner hooked upside down on the edge of the pool.

The game was fun, at least for a while. Nobody gave the girls much problem. When they got the ball, the boys just got in front of them, waved their arms, and forced the girls to pass the ball. Werner did try to take the ball away from Gertie, but I think he just wanted to get close to her.

I caught Fritz eying Hannah when he thought no one was looking.

Hannah and I hung back and held hands under water, whispering to each other about nothing special as the game rocked along at a leisurely summer pace.

A few minutes later, I got the ball on a pass from one of the baseball players. I held the ball over my head, bobbing up and down in the water, looking for a chance to pass off to Werner. I was just taking things easy, enjoying the water and the warm afternoon, my mind still on The Kiss in the Pantry and Hannah.

Then all of a sudden, Fritz went after me like we

had agreed to shoot the loser of the water polo match. He swarmed up in my face, grabbed my head with one hand, and pushed me under the water. I could feel his other hand slapping at my arm, trying to knock the ball free.

I barely had time to hold my breath and I fought and struggled to get my head above water. Fritz shoved me even further down. The ball slipped out of my hand. Fritz lunged for the bobbing soccer ball, kicking me in the chest as he shoved past me in pursuit of the ball.

Instinctively, I forced my way to the surface, gasping for breath. Just as instinctively, I went after the ball. I jumped on Fritz's back, pushed his head under the water, reached over him, and scooped up the ball. I pushed myself away from Fritz and looked for someone to pass to.

I spotted Werner in the middle of the pool, waving for the ball. I drew the ball back and got set to pass. But then I got torpedoed.

Fritz slammed into me and planted a hard right cross on my chin with his elbow. Little red rockets exploded in my head. Water gushed into my mouth and nose. The ball fell out of my hand.

I heard Hannah yelling.

Fritz ignored the ball and grabbed my shoulders with both hands and forced my head far down in the water. I felt disoriented and couldn't tell how far down I was. I was choking and struggling against Fritz's powerful grasp.

In desperation, instead of trying to pull away from Fritz, I struggled toward him and landed an elbow of my own square in the middle of his gut. His grip loosened and I fought my way to the surface.

Everyone was shouting and talking in German. Werner wrapped his arms around his friend and held him in a bear hug. Hannah guided me back toward the shallow end of the pool. I felt relieved when my feet touched the bottom, and I could stand up and fill my lungs with wonderful life-giving fresh air.

"This is not like Fritz," Hannah said. " I think the war has poisoned his mind. Oh, Ricky. I am so sorry."

"It's okay," I sputtered. "The game just got a little rough. I think Fritz is showing off for you. That's all."

Hannah got me out of the pool, and she and I sat down in a pair of wooden chairs in a grassy area off to the side. Fortunately, Werner quickly rounded up Gertie and Fritz and they headed for the bathhouse. The baseball players and the other girl got out of the pool and wrapped up in big towels and wandered back toward the compound houses. In a little while Werner, Gertie, and Fritz came out of the bathhouse in their clothes and took off down the road.

Fritz looked over his shoulder at me with a look that had revenge written all over it. I stared him down. Score one for the USA.

"Mein Gott," Hannah said. "Fritz has turned into such a hothead. Please forgive him."

"Sure. Why not?" I tried to smile.

Hannah leaned forward and stroked my arm. "I would not want anything to spoil this special, special day."

I looked up at her and grinned. "Neither would I," I

said. "It's all forgotten. Fritz is history."

Hannah took my hand, and we just sat there for a while. The departing sun dried our bodies and left our skin smelling of chlorine. Hannah gripped my hand like she wanted to keep our physical connection until Kingdom Come.

I was glad the ugly stuff that had happened between Fritz and me in the pool had not escalated any further. Besides the fact that the big German would probably have kicked my butt, I wanted the day to be about Hannah and me, not about some Nazi craphead and me.

The sun retreated slowly beyond the lake, and the mothers gathered up their little kids from the swimming pool, dried them off with oversized beach towels, and disappeared back into the residential section of the compound. Finally, Hannah and I were alone.

She had a white towel draped over her shoulders, and her damp hair clung to her face, changing the focus of her appearance to her perfect nose where the tiny army of freckles marched into infinity.

"I must be getting back soon," she said. "Meine Mutter will be serving the evening meal. Perhaps I will have time to give Fritz a—what do you Americans say? A piece of my brain."

"Mind. A piece of your mind. But don't do that. Fritz is a pretty dangerous character."

"Fritz is a little boy trying to play all grown up. He doesn't scare me. His behavior toward you was abominable," Hannah said.

"It's okay," I smiled. "As long as I wound up here

with you. Like this."

Hannah lowered her eyes. "Ja. Is nice."

And it was nice. Hannah and I all alone in the little grassy area between the swimming pool and the social hall with nothing to bother us. Nobody else around. It was one of those moments you wish could last forever and then some.

But she finally stood up. "I must go. They will be waiting for me."

I shrugged. I guess all good things must come to an end.

"You can dress in the bathhouse," Hannah's soapy scent remained despite the time in the pool. "No one is around. I'm sure Fritz won't return. He wouldn't dare."

"Can I come back to see you?" I held my breath waiting for her answer.

A shy smile crept across her face. "At the first opportunity, Ricky. Please. We . . . you and I—"

I pulled her close and kissed her again. Her lips were softer than velvet and tasted slightly like chlorine. I closed my eyes.

This was The Kiss by the Pool and was only slightly less wonderful than The Kiss in the Pantry. And then she was gone.

After Hannah left, I went into the bathhouse to get my clothes before heading home. Hannah told me to leave Werner's suit on the bench and somebody would come back and get it the next day.

The bald man in the blue suit was asleep in his chair by the staircase.

I peeled off the bathing suit, hopped in the shower

for a second, toweled off, retrieved my clothes from the open locker, and dressed quickly. The bathhouse was quiet except for the sound of a dripping faucet in the shower room and the uneven snores coming from the bald guy.

I hung Werner's suit on a nail, dropped my towel in the basket by the door, and headed toward the front door and the late afternoon sunshine.

But something stopped me. Loud voices coming in the front door of the locker room. Two guys speaking in rapid German. One voice was angry. Fritz and another guy were heading into the locker room. I didn't need Sherlock Holmes to figure out Fritz had come back looking for me, hoping to catch me alone when Hannah wasn't around.

I ducked behind a row of lockers, where the smell of mildew was overwhelming.

The loud voices woke up the man by the stairwell. He jumped out of his chair and headed for the entrance to the locker room, yelling something in German. It was "what the hell is going on?" in any language.

In a minute the bald guy and Fritz got into it, yelling at each other in German. I didn't know what they were saying, but I knew if Fritz and his buddy got me alone in the locker room my goose was cooked.

I snuck down the row of lockers. When I reached the end, I darted across the tile floor and sprinted up the metal staircase.

I paused at the top of the stairs to catch my breath and

let my heart slow down. Fear gripped my gut. The mildew smell was worse on the top floor. There was a big window on one side of the tiny room, but the window was closed and the place felt warm and cramped and musty like an attic in the summer heat. The window looked out on the pool and Lake Maracaibo in the distance. The water in the lake was calm and the setting sun sent shimmering streaks across the blue-green surface.

There were some cardboard boxes stacked in one corner of the cramped room and a beat-up old desk across from the window and some other stuff, but as my breath returned to normal I could only see one thing— the only thing in the room that mattered. A huge shortwave radio set, perched on a battered wooden table beside the window. The thing was half as tall as I was and had a dozen dials and buttons and switches. A pair of headphones lay idle on the table, surrounded by scraps of paper covered with hastily scrawled letters and numerals.

There it was, right out in the open—the radio Uncle Harry said the Germans in the compound used to contact the Nazi U-boats. The radio Old Mr. Taggert had found just before he was murdered.

The dying sun gave off a last bright beam and dust motes swirled in the light. I exhaled and bit down hard on my lower lip to keep it from trembling. The shouts from the locker room below grew louder.

Why wasn't the radio tucked away behind some secret panel or hidden deep in a cave or something? The shortwave was just sitting out in the open in the top floor of the bathhouse where anybody could find it. It wasn't even in a locked room.

Then it hit me. The bald man in the suit was a guard. He was guarding the stairway and the radio on the top floor. Having a radio set was not against the law. Anyone could have one. Creole Oil was an American company and America wasn't at war with Germany. The Germans in the compound were company employees. They could have a radio if they wanted. And besides, nobody other than the Germans ever came to the German compound anyway. And if anybody did come to the German compound, they sure wouldn't come for an afternoon dip in the pool and wouldn't have any business in the bathhouse. But they had posted a guard by the stairwell.

I guess it was even okay for the Germans to talk to the U-boats if they wanted. But somehow that sounded wrong and evil. And if Mr. Taggert had found the radio, I was sure some Nazi like Fritz or the bald guy in the suit had killed him because Mr. Taggert would tell the company and the German's secret would be out. Uncle Harry had been right.

I thought about doing my patriotic duty and smashing the radio.

I looked around for a hammer or something, but suddenly the angry voices echoed off the tile walls of the bathhouse locker room below. I jumped like I'd been shot. What if Fritz and his buddy came up to the top floor?

I did a quick sweep of the room, looking for a way out. There were no ledges outside the window. Just a straight drop to the gravel road below. There was no skylight.

I was trapped.

The voices got louder. They were speaking in German, barking out the words. "Find the little creep and kill him. Rip his limbs off. Slit his throat like the old man." I didn't understand a word of German, but I'm sure that's what they were saying.

I looked around for a weapon. A stick. A letter opener. A baseball bat. Anything.

I struck out again. No escape. No weapon.

The voices were right next to the stairwell. I flattened my body against the wall next to the radio. "Ja, vol, Yesrottzenhaimer." Or something like that. Then the voices moved away and grew faint.

I raced to the window and looked down at the pool. Fritz and another young man in a white shirt and dark slacks were talking to the bald guy in the suit. The guard gestured with his hands, indicating that Fritz and his friend should go away.

Fritz kept pointing at the bathhouse. The guard shook his head no. He planted his hand on his hip, pushing his suit coat back.

The guy was carrying a gun, a big black gun in a hip holster. I had snuck past an armed guard and found the German radio. My heart went crazy. How could one boy get himself into so much trouble?

I had to act quickly.

I sprinted back to the staircase and raced down the stairs, taking them two at a time. I rushed back through the locker room, away from the door. When I got to the back wall, I pulled a wooden bench over to the window. The window was open to let in the summer breeze. Hopping up on the bench, I put my hands on the windowsill and propelled myself through the window. I landed on the grass and rolled. A quick check let me know I hadn't broken any bones.

I looked around. I had landed behind the bathhouse. The main road around the pool area and headed for the main gate. The road was about twenty yards away. If I could get to the road and run for the gate I might be able to get away before Fritz and his buddy or the guard saw me.

Jesse Owens couldn't have caught me. I sprinted across the grass, hit the main road at a full gallop, and didn't slow down until I reached the main gate.

I ran out of the German compound, circled the big pipes and the bachelor barracks, scampered past the school ground, and raced down the dirt path toward the American compound. Puffing and panting, I didn't stop until I rounded the corner of our street and saw our house.

"Right this very minute, Creole Petroleum is producing over half of Venezuela's oil," my father said, lighting his pipe and watching the bluish smoke curl toward the sky.

"Yes, but at what cost?" Uncle Harry sprawled on the bench in front of us, his feet propped up on his green duffle bag. He had had the bag since The Great War. The duffle was scuffed and patched, the canvas handles threadbare. "Just a few years ago, a fire fueled by our surface runoff destroyed the whole village of Lagunillas. Gone. Poof. The whole place. How's that for progress?"

Daddy and Uncle Harry and I sat in the top deck of the ferryboat. Daddy was wearing his best white dress shirt and a blue tie. Uncle Harry had on a clean pair of black slacks and a pressed blue shirt. I had on clean khaki pants and a white sport shirt with a wide collar. The early morning sun was peeking over the horizon, hurling bolts of bright sunshine at the lake. The three of us were on our way to spend the day in Maracaibo.

I think Daddy was worried about me. I couldn't sleep and my appetite had gone south. I had a major case of the mopes and couldn't seem to shake 'em. Kissing Hannah had been so great, I could barely think about anything else. But then the shortwave radio on the top floor of the bathhouse kept pushing its way into my brain, taunting me, daring me to do something about it.

Only I didn't know what to do. I felt like I had to tell Daddy or somebody. The radio meant Uncle Harry was probably right about who had killed Mr. Taggert. I rehearsed in my mind yet again the events Uncle Harry said led up to Mr. Taggert having being murdered. Mr. Taggert had probably found the radio in the bathhouse just like I had, and one of the Germans—my money was on Fritz—had chased him out to the pipes and murdered him. So I needed to tell somebody what I had found. Guilt was crushing me.

I thought about telling Mama about the radio, but she had taken to drinking more and more at the Club while she played bridge. By the time she got home, she usually didn't make much sense.

I couldn't tell anybody else. I didn't know what the company might do to the Germans still living in the compound. I didn't know what they might do to Hannah and her family. If the company kicked all the Germans out of the camp, I'd probably never see Hannah again. So I just kept my mouth shut.

On the way to the ferry dock, Uncle Harry told Daddy there had been a sighting of a German U-boat just off the coast up in the Gulf of Venezuela just north of Lake Maracaibo, not that many miles from the Creole Camp. Maybe the Germans in the camp had used their radio to bring the U-boat there. But I didn't say a word. I just bit my lip and put my head down.

Anyway, for the past few days I'd been hanging around the house, trying to figure out a way to get back over to the German compound to see Hannah without running into Fritz and his gang. I couldn't do a lick of homework, and I think Mrs. Sullards talked to Mama over at the Club. So Daddy let me skip school and take the ferry over to Maracaibo, thinking the change in routine would do me good.

Daddy had to talk to some company people in the city about getting a bunch of new equipment for the rig and Uncle Harry went along to help.

My father and Uncle Harry kept up their never-ending conversation on the deck. "For God's sake, Harry," Daddy said. "Those were the frontier days. We're fixing all that now. Look at that lake. Clean as a whistle. We've cleaned up the sludge. Plus the derricks in the future will be even cleaner. We're learning."

Uncle Harry shook his head and grinned at me. "Your Daddy's forgotten where he comes from. He didn't always think the company was so benevolent. Time was he knew the company just wanted to stick it to the workingman. Now? I dunno."

"Come on, Harry. You're like Dixie's record player when it gets stuck. You just keep playing the same song over and over."

Uncle Harry nodded and smiled again. He and Daddy had been having the same conversation for years. I think it was fun for both of them. "Well, I'd love to stay here and debate the evils of capitalism with you gentlemen," Uncle Harry said. "But I've got a date down below with a pair of lucky ladies that are gonna win us a fine lunch in the best restaurant in Maracaibo." He stood up, hoisted the heavy duffle bag over his shoulder with a groan, tipped his fedora, and headed for the stairs.

Daddy repacked his pipe, tucked the stem in his mouth, and thoughtfully gnawed on the wood. "The man is the worst gambler in the western hemisphere," he said out of the corner of his mouth. "I reckon I'll have to buy his lunch and spot him enough cash to make it to payday. Some things never change." He let out a little chuckle.

I smiled a little even as a voice somewhere deep in my head screamed, "Tell him! Tell Daddy about the radio! You have to tell him! This is important! Tell him!" But the moment passed. Daddy gnawed on his pipe, and we looked out over the whitecaps on the lake, watching the camp fade in the distance. I just couldn't do it. I knew I should, but I couldn't. I was afraid if I said the words out loud it would make it all true: the radio was being used to make war, to hurt and kill innocent people. If I told Daddy, it would get Hannah and her family in a bunch of trouble and that was the last thing in the world I wanted to do.

A few minutes later, Daddy put his pipe back in his shirt pocket, cocked his fedora on the back of his head, and said, "I bet you and me could rustle up a Coca-Cola and a cup of coffee somewhere on this tub if we had half a mind to. What d'you say?"

"Sure. That'd be great."

There were only a handful of other passengers on the deck, mostly men from the company like Daddy, heading across the lake on business. Daddy nodded at them as we made our way to the stairway heading down to the lower deck.

Downstairs, Daddy found the young man who had taken our tickets when we got on the ferry. He was blond and wore a white shirt and a tie. Daddy asked him where we might get coffee and a Coca-Cola. The man said there was a fresh pot of coffee in the alcove by the door and some sodas in the icebox below the counter. He said the old fellow behind the counter would take our money.

Daddy got a cup of coffee in a white mug and handed me a cold bottle of Coca-Cola, and we started back for the upper deck when Daddy spotted a handful of Venezuelan natives sitting on benches lining the right side of the lower deck. "There's Renaldo and Jovito," he said. "They're on my crew out on the rig. I need to have a word with them."

I shrugged and took a swig of my Coke. Daddy started toward the men.

"Hold it there, Mr. Ches." The blond man all but sprinted across the lower deck. "I don't think you want to go down that way. That's the natives' seating area. White folks don't go in there. And the Venezuelans don't go up on the upper deck. That's the way we do things here."

Daddy stopped, blew on his coffee to cool it, and then took a sip from the mug. "Oh, it's no problem," he said. "I just need to ask a couple of those fellows about some new equipment we're about to buy. See what they think would work best. Then I'll head on up top. It's nothing to worry about."

"Sir, I'd rather you didn't," the blond man said. "The company doesn't like our white people fraternizing with the natives. The big wigs at Creole don't like that at all."

Daddy filled his cheeks with air and then blew the air out of his mouth all at once. "Well, I reckon you work for the company and I work for the company and those fellows in there work for the company, so I guess we are the company. So I don't see a problem, okay?"

The blond man looked confused. "Sir, I just can't allow white people to go in there and socialize with the natives. That's against company policy."

Daddy took another sip of coffee. "Son, I'm going in there and I'm gonna talk to those fellows and sit a spell and finish my coffee. I don't rightly see there's a whole lot you can do about it. So if you'll excuse me. Come on, Ricky."

I followed Daddy into the native section of the ferryboat. The blond man planted his hands on his hips and watched us go. His face burned crimson. Daddy was right. There wasn't a whole lot he could do about it.

Inside the native section, the men Daddy had called Renaldo and Jovito looked like they had seen a ghost when we walked in. They both grabbed their hats off their heads and stood up, looking nervously around. Renaldo was a young man with stooped shoulders and dark skin. Jovito was older and shorter and had a pencil thin salt-and-pepper mustache.

Daddy motioned them to sit down and found a seat on a bench across from them. He motioned for me to sit beside him. My father spoke passable Spanish and started talking to Renaldo and Jovito. After a while the two men relaxed.

I figured out they were talking about some kind of machine. Or at least parts of some machine. The two Venezuelans seemed interested in the machine and they started talking and gesturing with their hands, explaining the workings of the mysterious machine, which apparently turned clockwise and then quickly turned counterclockwise.

I sipped my Coca-Cola and started daydreaming about Hannah Oudt. Then the shortwave radio in the bathhouse shoved its way into my mind.

Daddy waved his pipe around enthusiastically at whatever they were saying and made a bunch of hand gestures of his own. Jovito vigorously shook his head no, said a bunch of Spanish, and made a gesture of his own. It was like Daddy's motion only his hands rotated in the opposite direction. Daddy smiled and nodded his agreement.

This went on until the ferry docked at Maracaibo. Men who love machines, no matter what language they speak, can talk about machines forever. But as things turned out, Daddy, Jovito, and Renaldo were actually talking about something else that day on the ferry.

The hustle and bustle of Maracaibo was another

universe from the quiet pace across the lake in the Creole Camp. Everyone in the city seemed in a hurry. And every place you went new smells assaulted your senses—spicy food, unwashed bodies, gasoline, flowers, you name it.

Daddy and Uncle Harry found a cab. The driver, a dark-haired native missing most of his front teeth, wove his way through the narrow streets, one hand on the horn, honking at cars that cut in front of him or donkey-pulled carts that were too slow to clear the street. He alternately floored the accelerator and then stomped on the brake petal. Daddy and Uncle Harry and I slid around in the backseat, laughing the whole way.

The cab finally screeched to a halt in front of an office building with "Creole Petroleum Company" in gold letters on the frosted glass of the front door. Two gold spittoons flanked the door.

Daddy paid the cab driver and then gave me fifty cents. He said I could hang around in the marketplace across the street from the Creole building while he and Uncle Harry conducted their business.

I took the money and hustled across the street.

The marketplace was flanked by brightly colored stucco walls, which separated the houses behind them from the noise and activity of the busy street. Most of the walls were covered with tropical vines that were in full blossom with red, yellow, or white flowers, which in turn provided a perfumed curtain that surrounded the market.

Wild birds flocked to the tops of the walls, adding their brilliant plumage and shrill songs to the rumble of open-air commerce. Cramped stalls exhibited jade jewelry and bright blankets and lace and bananas and mangoes and oranges and melons and pies and Stetsons and broad sombreros. Deeply tanned men, with droopy eyelids, sat on canvas chairs in the rear of the stalls. At the far end of the marketplace was a tiny plaza with a fountain in the center, guarded by a potbellied stone angel that stood in the center of the fountain, a whimsical grin on his chubby face.

I found a guy selling sodas out of a big red cooler and had my second Coca-Cola of the day. Any day that you have two Coca-Colas has got to be a good day.

After a couple of hours, Daddy and Uncle Harry caught up with me back in the market. I was watching this guy in a stall cut up dead chickens with a cleaver. His hands moved so fast they were hard to follow. He'd whip the chicken around with one hand and then hack it with the cleaver. It was like a little show.

As my father, Uncle Harry, and I walked a few blocks to a place Uncle Harry had heard about, Daddy and Uncle Harry rehashed their morning meeting with the company bosses. Apparently things had gone well, and they were going to get the new equipment for the derricks. Both of them were excited because the new machines would really increase oil production on the lake.

Daddy bought all of us hamburgers and french fries in an American drugstore that had a soda fountain. I had my third Coca-Cola of the day, which made the day something really special.

"Tell you what," Uncle Harry said, wiping his

mouth on his napkin. "The last ferry won't be pulling out until just before dark. I think I'll do a little sightseeing and maybe some shopping and—"

"That's a great idea," my father said. "Maybe you could take Ricky along with you. I've got to meet with Lattimore and Jenkins about the drilling cables and that's gonna take most of the afternoon. You wouldn't mind, would you, Harry?"

Uncle Harry pursed his lips together, and I could tell he did mind but he didn't want to say anything. He pressed his tongue into his cheek. "Uh, no. No. That'd be fine. Me and Ricky will have us an adventure or two. Right, lad?"

"You bet." Whatever Uncle Harry and I did would be more fun than going with my father to some boring meeting. Uncle Harry was always fun.

And that's how I wound up at the cockfights.

The bouts were held in a cheaply constructed warehouse on the edge of Maracaibo. By the time Uncle Harry and I got there, the place was packed. Rough-looking men in dirty shirts with bandanas around their necks crowded in next to respectable looking businessmen who wore suits and ties and smelled of bay rum. Everyone was talking in loud, excited voices, cigarettes dangling from the corners of their mouths. A thick cloud of smoke hung over the sand-filled circle in the center of the warehouse.

"Best we don't be telling your papa where we spent the afternoon," Uncle Harry said, winking at me as we waded into the crowd. He swung the shoulder strap of the heavy duffle bag around his neck so the bag rode on his back like a hiker's backpack. "Best we keep this our little secret, agreed?"

I nodded, feeling enormously grown-up and excited about our adventure.

An old man wearing a battered cowboy hat was raking the sandpit as we found a spot near the edge of the circle, next to a bunch of men who needed a bath in the worst way.

The electricity in the air escalated. Everyone began yelling in Spanish as a young man with a white streak in his hair strutted into the pit, carrying an enormous white rooster in both arms.

In just a few seconds, a dark-skinned older man entered the circle with a red rooster on his shoulder.

The audience went wild, yelling and screaming. A dozen men in identical white fedoras with bright red hatbands circulated through the crowd. They tossed small leather bags back and forth to various men, who stuffed folded Venezuelan money into the bags and flashed unintelligible hand signals to the men in the red-banded hats. The hand gestures reminded me of a third base coach flashing signals to a batter in a baseball game.

Leather bags flew all over the arena like wingless birds.

Uncle Harry flashed a couple of signs and then caught the leather bag like a center fielder. "This is gonna make up for the lousy dice on the boat," he laughed. He stuffed a wad of cash in the bag and let me toss it back to one of the guys in the red-banded hats.

When the bets were down, the trainers placed their roosters in the center of the sandpit and backed away. The cocks eyed each other, their combs erect. Then they charged and the arena exploded with an avalanche of screaming and yelling and cheering and stomping and shouting.

The cocks used their beaks like knives, stabbing wildly at their opponent. Their spurs tore their enemy's flesh away in huge gashes until both birds were covered with blood. Feathers filled the air.

Suddenly I didn't feel grown-up at all. I just felt sick to my stomach.

The white rooster collapsed. The younger trainer took a big swig from a bottle of vinegar and spewed the fiery liquid over the poor bird's injuries in an effort to force the pitiful creature to fight again. The wounded animal shook himself and tried to get up, but he just didn't have any more fight in him.

Uncle Harry had been cheering wildly, shaking his fist in the air. But then his face fell. He must have bet on the white bird. I lowered my head and checked out the tops of my shoes. Tears filled my eyes, and I rubbed my sockets with the backs of my hands to make the tears go away. I wasn't about to cry like some little kid in front of all those men, but geez, what kind of people enjoyed something that mean and cruel?

The men in the red-banded hats circulated through the crowd, tossing the tiny leather bags back and forth. Uncle Harry caught another bag, stuffed it with cash, and let me toss it back. He was smiling again. I took a deep breath and looked away from the blood-soaked sandpit.

"Ah," Uncle Harry said. "There's my appointment. Right on time. Come on, Sport." He put his thick, callused hands on my shoulders, and steered me through the crowd, which was already starting to buzz about the next fight. I never looked back.

Uncle Harry waved to a man in the back of the arena and the unsmiling man waved back. I recognized Inspector Caesar, the Venezuelan policeman who was investigating Mr. Taggert's murder. Apparently, Uncle Harry had set up some kind of meeting with the inspector at the cockfights. That seemed pretty weird to me.

The two men shook hands and Inspector Caesar nodded at me. I nodded back. The policeman's hair and mustache seemed even whiter than I remembered at the Club the morning after Hannah and I found Mr. Taggert's body in the pipe. The inspector's suit was neatly pressed and his white shirt was crisp and starched despite the heat and humidity in the arena.

"It's good of you to come, Inspector," Uncle Harry said. "Your office seemed a bit public if you know what I mean."

"I understand," the policeman said, still not smiling. "And, besides, I am a devoted fan of the cockfights. My one vice."

Uncle Harry shook his head. "Okay," he said, getting right down to business. "I wanted to meet with you about the investigation of the murder of Mr. Taggert over in the Creole Camp."

Inspector Caesar nodded, not wanting to speak over the sudden roar of the crowd behind us. The next two roosters had arrived in the sandpit.

"As I'm sure you know," Uncle Harry raised his voice to be heard over the roar, "our Security Chief in the camp is bent and determined to nail one or more of the native workers that Taggert fired for his murder. You know what I mean?"

The crowd quieted down, waiting for the roosters to go to war.

"That does seem to be Senior Long's assessment of the situation."

Uncle Harry let out a long sigh and shook his head. "Well, I'm here to tell you that I don't buy that those fellows killed Old Man Taggert. Not for a minute. No, sir."

Inspector Caesar's eyebrows rose slowly. "And why is that?"

"For one thing, Ricky's dad and I worked closely with those men." Uncle Harry rested his hands on my shoulders. "They were good workers. Hard working, sober men. Family men. Not the type to commit a violent murder. No, sir. They just didn't seem like the type."

Caesar made a clicking sound with his tongue. "I am inclined to agree with you, my friend. After a thorough investigation, I am virtually certain that none of those men returned to the Creole Camp the night in question. I would stake my badge on it."

Uncle Harry smiled. "Ricky's dad talked to some other native workers on the ferry this morning. They all swear the men who got fired had nothing to do with the murder."

"You and Senior Parker are most kind to take such an interest."

"Right, but that's not why I'm here. That's not what I need to tell you."

Caesar nodded. "Go on."

"Here's the way I see it." Uncle Harry leaned forward and lowered his voice. "We've got a bunch of Germans still working for the company and still living in the company compound over in the camp. See?"

My stomach lurched, and the sudden nausea didn't have anything to do with the bloody roosters that were ripping each other to shreds behind me. Oh, please, Uncle Harry, don't tell him. Please don't.

"A lot of us figure these Germans have got a shortwave radio stashed somewhere in their compound and they're talking to the Nazi U-boats up in the Caribbean. Sending secret information or some such."

"And?"

"And some of us figure Old Man Taggert found the radio and then skedaddled as quick as he could, but one of the German fellows chased him down and killed him so he wouldn't tell anybody about the radio. I bet you dollars to donuts that's exactly what happened."

My head was swimming. What was I gonna do? I was a loyal American who wanted to do the right thing. I knew right where the radio was. I could tell them exactly where to find the shortwave. But if I told, what would they do to the Germans in the camp? Would they send them home? Would they send Hannah back to

Germany, where I'd never see her again?

Behind me, the roosters shrieked in agony. I felt dizzy. My mouth fell open, but nothing came out.

Inspector Caesar looked grim and nodded at Uncle Harry. "Well, Senior, I appreciate your coming forth and telling me this. It sheds a whole different light on the case. If your theory proves correct, you have saved innocent men from much difficulty. You are clearly a man of character and I thank you."

I closed my eyes to keep from looking at the roosters in the pit. When I finally looked up Inspector Caesar was nowhere in sight. "Wait right here, Ricky," Uncle Harry said. "I've got one more piece of business. It'll just take a sec. Then I'll circle back and pick you up. Okay?"

"Sure."

"Don't leave this spot, got it?"

"I got it." Bombs couldn't have moved me from the spot.

Uncle Harry gave my shoulder a squeeze and wandered off toward the back of the arena.

I stood around, watching the men bet on the roosters and tried not to look into the pit where the birds were battling again. Finally I got worried about Uncle Harry. He'd been gone a long time. I finally abandoned my spot and wandered around the arena until I spotted Uncle Harry talking to a dark-skinned man in a neatly pressed business suit.

They were huddled together at the back of the arena, their heads close together. Relieved at finding Uncle Harry, I stopped next to a concrete pillar and took a deep breath. Behind me, the crowd screamed and yelled and stomped their feet. The whole place smelled like a barnyard.

Uncle Harry pulled his duffle bag off his shoulder. He unzipped the bag, glanced around, and pulled out what looked like a pair of small brown bottles. He held them up so the man could read the labels. The man nodded and Uncle Harry dropped the bottles back into the bag. Then he pulled out something else. The man grabbed Uncle Harry's hand and forced the object back into the duffle bag.

I shrank back behind the pillar.

The roar of the crowd grew louder.

Suddenly I felt a burning sensation race down my right arm and then something bumped me into the pillar. I whirled around and found myself face-to-face with a short, squat man with a big nose and a tiny mustache. He had a cowboy hat pulled low over his eyes.

I jumped back.

The man held a paper cup of steaming coffee in each hand. He let out a stream of Spanish that in any language meant he was sorry. He gestured toward the cockfighting ring with his head and held up the coffee. He motioned toward my arm and looked concerned.

Apparently he had been heading toward the ring, bringing coffee for himself and someone else, gotten distracted by the cockfight, walked right into me and spilled coffee on my arm.

My arm hurt a little and was turning red but I wasn't seriously burned. I pointed at my arm and gave the man the okay sign.

His face broke into a relieved grin.

"It's okay, see." I moved my arm around to demonstrate that everything was fine.

The man smiled some more, nodded, and backed away. He quickly disappeared into the crowd.

I looked more closely at my arm. The redness was already fading. I moved out from behind the pillar and headed for Uncle Harry.

Uncle Harry saw me walking across the arena floor and quickly shook hands with the man in the business suit. The man nodded and picked up a large, stylish athletic bag. It was dark blue with white trim and looked like the bags tennis players used to carry their gear. The bag was heavy and the man had trouble getting the strap up on his shoulder.

Uncle Harry said adios and flipped his own duffle bag over his shoulder. The businessman said something else, but the roar of the crowd drowned him out. Another one of the roosters bit the dust. The man shrugged and hurried out the exit.

≪ 16 ≫

Uncle Harry and I caught a cab outside the cockfight arena and headed back into Maracaibo. I couldn't talk. All I could do was stare out the window and gnaw on my lower lip. I didn't know what to do. I mean I knew I should tell Uncle Harry or my father about the radio in the bathhouse. Any idiot would know that.

The more I thought about it, the more Uncle Harry's idea about the Germans killing old Mr. Taggert made sense. If they really were using the radio to report important information to the Nazi submarines then they probably would kill someone to protect their evil secret. Fritz would for sure. So would the bathhouse guard. But still . . . if I told, what would they do to the Germans? Would the company send them all back to the Fatherland? Would I wake up one morning and find out that Hannah was gone forever? I couldn't stand the thought. So I just stared and gnawed.

We caught up with my father outside the Creole building.

"So did you fellows have a good time?" Daddy asked, lighting his pipe.

"Sure. Yeah. Swell." I still had trouble talking.

"This is a heck of a town, Chester. A heck of a town." Uncle Harry winked at me. "Tell you what. We've still got a couple of hours before the ferry leaves, and I've got a big surprise. You two up to one last adventure?"

"I reckon we are," my father said.

And we were off again.

We caught another cab and Uncle Harry handed a slip of paper to the driver, whose thin face lit up like a Christmas tree. Big fare. Daddy asked Uncle Harry what was going on, but Uncle Harry laughed and said we'd find out soon enough. He was clearly enjoying his little surprise.

The cab wound its way through the heavy Maracaibo traffic and finally headed north on a paved but deeply potholed road. We rambled past some tiny houses with dirt yards filled with poor children in raggedy clothes. Just like the Mississippi delta back home.

We even passed a little settlement of big packing crates that served as houses for some more raggedy children with dirt-smeared faces who were playing in the muddy road that fronted their crate village. One thing was for sure, oil money wasn't doing these people any good.

A couple of miles later the houses got a little nicer. They had palm trees in the front of trimmed yards. There weren't as many children.

The cab driver slowed down and finally pulled to a stop in front of a shabby gas station. The weather-beaten pumps in front sold "Super Venzuelan" gas. The place looked deserted.

"Harry, what in the world are you up to?" My father didn't know whether to laugh or fuss at Uncle Harry. "The ferry leaves in a hour or so. What in tarnation?"

Uncle Harry grinned. "Tell the driver to wait. You're gonna need a ride back to the ferry dock."

"And what are you gonna do?"

"You'll see. Just tell him to wait."

Daddy spoke to the driver in Spanish.

The three of us got out of the cab and Uncle Harry went inside the station while Daddy and I stood around in front of the dilapidated gas pumps, looking at the palm trees across the road. It was much cooler away from the city, and a gentle breeze made things almost pleasant.

Uncle Harry came out, accompanied by a little man with dark hair and a Pancho Villa mustache. They started walking around the station toward the back of the building and Uncle Harry motioned for Daddy and me to follow.

"Uncle Harry is half crazy," Daddy said under his breath. "Don't ever forget that."

I laughed. I hoped someday I'd have a friendship like the one Daddy and Uncle Harry had.

We hiked around to the back of the gas station and stopped short.

Uncle Harry was beaming from ear to ear, standing in front of a black Harley Davidson 50 cc motorbike. Talk about the cat's pajamas. The chrome handles of the bike shimmered in the late afternoon sun, and the black leather seat, although cracked, had been recently cleaned with saddle soap and looked like the comfortable palm of a well-oiled baseball glove.

"What d'you think? Is she a beauty or what? Jovito from the camp says Mr. Marchon here is the best cycle mechanic in Venezuela. The bike's got some miles on it, but Mr. Marchon says she runs like a top."

"You're not thinking of buying this thing, are you?" Daddy stuck his pipe in the corner of his mouth.

"Not anymore." Uncle Harry couldn't stop grinning. He reached into his pants pocket, pulled out a thick wad of bills, counted out a bunch of them, and handed the money to Mr. Marchon. "I've already bought her. She's mine free and clear."

"Where in God's name did you get . . .?"

"Lady Luck's been with me over in the barracks the last couple of nights. Stud poker. Best game man ever invented. Not to mention what I won coming over on the ferry this morning." Uncle Harry gave me a quick wink before he burst out laughing. The cockfights were our secret.

Daddy shook his head.

Uncle Harry hopped into the saddle of the motorbike and bounced up and down. Mr. Marchon slipped back around the side of the gas station. Daddy and I stood there staring at Uncle Harry's new toy, all power and leather and chrome.

"Here's what we'll do," Uncle Harry said. "Ches, you take the cab back to the ferry dock and Ricky and I will take the motorbike. I bet you a five spot we beat you there."

"You . . . mean it?" The prospect of riding the cycle back to the dock was the most exciting idea I'd heard in a long time.

"Sure." Uncle Harry kick-started the Harley. The engine roared and white smoke puffed out of the tailpipe. He revved the engine even louder. No kid could ever be happier with his presents on Christmas morning than Uncle Harry was with his new motorbike.

Mr. Marchon reappeared and handed Uncle Harry a pair of goggles. At that moment, Daddy's best friend in the whole world, perched on the motorbike with his shaved head and goggles, looked just like a character out of a Doc Savage novel, ready to fight the evildoers wherever he might find them. And I was gonna ride with him.

"Hop on," Uncle Harry called to me over the din of the engine roar.

I looked at Daddy. He was fighting a losing battle with a smile of his own. He nodded and I jumped on the bike behind Uncle Harry.

"I'll meet you two adventurers back at the dock," Daddy said. He waved and headed toward the waiting cab.

Uncle Harry revved down the engine. "Here's the setup," he said, looking back over his shoulder. "You work the clutch with this hand and shift gears down here." He clicked a thick metal strip up and down with his foot. "First is up one. Second is down two. Third is down three. The throttle is right here on the handlebars. Clutch on the left, throttle on the right. It's simple." He revved up the engine again. "And these are the brakes."

He squeezed the grips on the handlebars. "I'll let you drive her when we get back to the camp."

"Oh, man, Uncle Harry. Thanks." I had to shout over the engine. Uncle Harry was the best.

Rummm! Rummmm! Uncle Harry twisted the throttle.

When we got back to the Creole Camp, I'd have to do the gearshift operation that Uncle Harry just told me. And I hadn't paid any attention to what he said. That was the way machines affected me. Mention nuts, bolts, screws, gears, or whatever, and my mind raced off somewhere.

Rummm! Rummm!

The ride back to the ferry dock was the most fun ever. Uncle Harry had obviously been on a bike before. He crouched over the handlebars and leaned into the curves, shifting his weight to steady the motorbike. He gave the cycle full throttle on the straightaway, and the Venezuelan countryside and the shanties and the poor children flew past us.

I hung on to Uncle Harry's waist and reveled in the sheer joy of the ride, the wind in my hair and on my face, and the thrill of speed on the open road. The ride on Uncle Harry's motorbike was so wonderfully fun that, for a brief moment, the speed and the curves and the passing countryside made me forget that I was still guarding the secret of the Germans' radio in the bathhouse.

And what a mistake that was.

≪ 17 ≫

I woke up early Sunday morning just as the sun's first grayish glimmer crept into my bedroom. I usually slept late on Sunday, but I was too excited to sleep. Or maybe too nervous. This was the day Uncle Harry was gonna teach me to ride the motorbike.

I could do it. I knew I could. Uncle Harry would walk me through it. He would show me how to shift the gears, work the throttle, and the other stuff on the motorbike. I didn't have to be great at it. I just had to be able to do it.

After Uncle Harry showed me how to work the machine, I was gonna ride the bike over to the German compound and pick up Hannah. And then she and I could go riding the back roads around the Creole Camp. I hadn't seen her in almost a week. But today would be the day. I had to see Hannah or I'd go crazy.

I got up, put on my bathrobe, and went into the living room. It was the first week of December, and Mama had unpacked a small box of Christmas tree decorations—tinsel, red and green decorative balls, and a star for the top of the tree. The decorations blanketed the dining room table. The company had promised to get a load of Christmas trees from the states to the Creole Camp in time for Christmas. Mama loved Christmas, and she was ready for the tree to arrive.

I was sick of powdered milk, so I went into the kitchen, made myself a couple of pieces of toast, ladled grape jelly all over them, and wolfed them down. Then I curled up with a couple of comics in the big chair in the living room.

Mama and Daddy got up a little later. They had coffee and cigarettes around the kitchen table and reread a paper from three or four days ago. Daddy looked tired. His face was drawn and his eyes were ringed with dark circles. Things weren't going well out on the rigs.

Around noon I heard the roar of Uncle Harry's motorbike cutting through the Sunday morning stillness, getting closer and closer. My stomach flipped. This was it. Gears or not, I could do it. I just knew I could. I hustled back into my room, put on a pair of black pants and a green shirt, and checked my hair in the mirror.

Mama heard the bike and got up to put on the percolator to make another pot of coffee. Daddy lit his pipe.

The roar of Uncle Harry's engine got louder and louder, and then the bike was right in front of our house. Uncle Harry cut the engine, and the silence sounded strange and harsh.

Uncle Harry always knocked on our kitchen door with the familiar "Shave and a Haircut, Six Bits," but that morning he attacked the door with his fist. Bam!

Bam! Bam!

And somehow I knew in the next couple of minutes everything was about to change. And never change back.

"For God's sake, Harry." Mama headed for the kitchen door. "You're gonna wake the dead." Before she could get the door open all the way, Uncle Harry burst into the room. His face was flushed crimson with excitement. His eyes were wide like the mad scientist in the Commando Cody serials back in El Dorado. He was wearing a wrinkled work shirt and a pair of work pants.

"Harry, what is it?" Mama closed the door behind him.

"The Japs!" Uncle Harry was out of breath. "They bombed Pearl Harbor! Out in Hawaii. Early this morning. Hundreds of Jap planes. Outta nowhere. Thousands of our guys killed. Big Mike Thompson picked up the news on his shortwave from the radio over in Caracas. This is the real thing. The Japs attacked us!"

Daddy's hand trembled as he set his coffee cup down on the kitchen table. "The Japanese," he said. "Not the Germans? The Japanese?"

"Don't worry, we'll be at war with the Germans too before nightfall. It's happened. It's finally happened. We're at war."

My father shook his head in sorrow and disbelief.

"Y'all come on. We gotta get going." Uncle Harry danced around the living room, too excited to sit down.

Mama stood frozen by the door, her face ashen, her hands clutched to her chest.

"Come on, get a move on." Uncle Harry nervously wiped his mouth on the back of his hand. "The natives are acting crazy. They've heard the news. They know everything is topsy-turvy. A bunch of them have wandered over from their compound. Some of them are carrying machetes. John Moore says to get all the women and children up to the Club. Big Mike and Sid Jones and some of the boys have got their shooting irons ready. They're gonna stand guard at the Club."

"What about the rigs?" Daddy snapped out of his daze.

"I reckon we need to get out there as soon as we can."

"Let's find Renaldo and Jovito and some of those fellows first. Talk to them. See what's going on."

I was standing in the doorway, my hands thrust deep into my pockets, desperately trying to understand what was going on. "What . . . what about the Germans? Over in their compound."

Uncle Harry barely looked at me. "Ernie Martin and Bob Wiggins and some of those fellows broke out their shotguns and they're heading over to Germantown right this minute. We won't have any trouble there. Come on, Dixie. Throw on some clothes quick. Ches, get your rifle. I don't like the looks of things. I'll take the bike and circle by the barracks and get my gun, and I'll meet y'all at the Club. Hurry now."

And Uncle Harry was gone. I heard the roar of the motorbike fading into the distance.

Mama and Daddy threw on their clothes. As we headed out the front door, Mama turned around and raced back into the dining room, where she dug into the top drawer of the cabinet and pulled out a small silver flask and a deck of playing cards. She dropped the cards and the flask into her purse and rushed out the door.

The three of us started up the street to the Club, but we stopped a couple of times to briefly speak to neighbors who were coming out of their houses, looking startled and confused. Some of the women had been crying, tear tracks and red eyes were everywhere. No one had any more news. Everyone hugged.

As we approached the Club, the atmosphere changed. The tension was so great you could almost reach out and touch it. Like Uncle Harry said, the native workers were walking around the camp in twos and threes. Some of them did have machetes in their hands and all of them had knives tucked in their belts. They were scowling and sullen looking. They didn't seem to want anything or have a destination. They were just walking around, looking scary.

A pair of American men in Stetson hats stood in front of the Club, shotguns riding in the crooks of their arms. They glared warily at the natives almost daring the Venezuelans to try something.

The Club was packed. Women with no makeup, many of them in house dresses they would never have worn in public, herded small children in front of them and talked to each other in loud, excited voices. Some of the kids from my class at the Creole Camp school stood around awkwardly in one corner, not knowing what to say to each other.

There were no men inside the Club.

Daddy stopped at the door. "I want you to stay here and look after your mother," he said quietly. "I wish you could go with us. I think you could help. But I just can't leave your mother here by herself. I need you to watch out for her."

"Yessir." It was not the time to argue with my father.

"I'm gonna hook up with Harry and see if we can find out what's going on. I'll be back as soon as I can. I'm sure things are okay. Everybody's just all riled up right now. Things will settle down. In the meantime, keep your eyes open." Daddy gave my shoulder a hard squeeze.

I nodded and he was gone.

Inside the Club, Mama hugged several of the women. All the chairs in the Club were filled. Everyone else milled around and talked and talked and hugged and cried. It was hot and stuffy in the packed building.

I spotted Sonny and Will Cole over in the corner. Their eyes were wide with fear and their mother sat hunched over in a chair, cupping her face in her hands, her body wracked with sobs. Tess and Bess, the twins from the school, ran around talking to anyone in the Club who would listen to them.

The Great Room of the Club seemed alive with the loud droning of dozens of conversations. Rumors flew thicker than flies.

After a while, Mama found me standing by myself, staring out the window of the Club, looking at nothing. She put her arm around my shoulder and pulled me close to her.

The hug felt good.

"It's not supposed to be this way," Mama said. "We should be living back in the house in El Dorado. You should be playing baseball with your friends, doing your homework at the kitchen table, and later on, going to dances with pretty young girls. No economic upheaval, no company camp, no dead bodies, no wars. I'm sorry, Ricky. None of this was supposed to happen."

I slipped my arm around Mama's waist and hugged her back. "I guess we can't always make everything turn out the way we want," I said, thinking about Hannah as much as anything.

"We sure can't," Mama said. "But we still have each other. Me and you and your father. And that's what matters. That we're together. Together we can face anything."

I couldn't add anything to that, so I just stood there and held my mother while she held me. We stared out the window of the Club, trying to see the future.

After a few minutes, Mr. Moore, the supervisor who had replaced Mr. Taggert, came into the club through the back door. He made his way to the center of the room, jumped up on one of the heavy bridge tables, and held up his hands to get everyone's attention.

The room went silent.

"Folks, I need to have a word with you." Mr. Moore, who was a thickset man with a deep Texas twang, didn't bother to remove his fedora. His white shirt was damp with sweat. "I know all of you are worried and a little scared. I'm gonna give you all the information I can. We've got a pretty powerful radio over at the administration building, and Darcy McCormick is monitoring it, trying to pick up what news he can out of Caracas and Maracaibo. So far what we know is that Japanese airplanes attacked the American fleet at Pearl Harbor early this morning and did a lot of damage. We know that a lot of brave young American boys lost their lives in the attack. God bless 'em all."

Several women in the Club crossed themselves. Several others mumbled "amen."

"Closer to home, the news of the attack has riled up some of the native workers. I don't think they know exactly what all this means, but they know some kind of war is about to commence. Chester Parker has talked to some of their leaders. They trust Mr. Ches. He's a good man and he's treated 'em right. They'll listen to him. Anyway, he's talked most of them into going on home for the day."

People turned their heads and looked at Mama and me. Daddy had saved the day, at least for a while.

"Can we go on home soon?" A woman in a print dress called out.

"In a little while, Maybelle. Soon as we're sure everything is all right."

"Are we at war?" Another woman in the corner of the Club called out, and a murmur ran through the crowd.

"Well, I reckon we are." Mr. Moore pulled out a blue bandana and mopped his face.

"Are we at war with the Germans as well as the Japs?" someone else shouted.

"I'm not sure." Mr. Moore stuffed his bandana back in his pocket. "But my best guess is we will be pretty soon. I'm guessing in the next day or two the United States is gonna jump into the war with both feet."

"What about the Germans right here in the Camp?" The woman named Maybelle called out, angry venom dripping with her voice.

My heart leaped into my throat.

"Yeah, what about them? What are we gonna do about them?"

"The hell with the Germans. And the Japs too!"

Loud applause filled the Club.

Mr. Moore waved his hands to quiet the crowd. "Well, I do have some news for you on that count." He let out a long sigh.

Murmurs continued to run through the crowd.

"Early this morning," the new supervisor raised his voice above the din, "as soon as I found out about the attack at Pearl, Darcy McGregor and Leon Finch and me and a couple of other fellows got our guns and ran over to the German compound. But folks, let me tell you, and this here is really amazing—all the Germans are gone. Every one of them. Every German worker in the camp up and vanished in the night. I swear that's the Lord's gospel truth. All of 'em. Up and gone."

The crowd exploded. Everyone turned and started talking to the people near them in loud, concerned voices. Everyone had an opinion.

Gone. Vanished. All of them.

The cramped, stuffy room started spinning. Gone. Hannah was gone. Vanished. Werner and Mrs. Oudt and little Hans. Gone. I pressed my hands against my temples to make the room stop spinning.

"What d'you mean, gone?" A woman in the back of the club yelled.

"Just what I said," Mr. Moore replied. "Gone. It looks like somehow they got word of the Jap attack before anybody else, threw a few belongings into their suitcases, and took off."

Got word of the attack? I knew what that meant. The radio in the bathhouse. It had to be. I thought the blood pounding into my brain might make my head explode.

"Where'd they go? The ferry boat don't run at night."

"That's true," Mr. Moore said. "Best we can figure is the Germans hightailed it up into the hills somewhere."

My brain regained its focus. The U-boats! The Germans from the camp were waiting for the U-boats to pick them up! I just knew it. The U-boats would take them back to Germany. I'd never see Hannah again. My mouth turned into a desert that was so dry I couldn't swallow. Hannah Oudt was gone forever.

"How are they gonna live up there?"

"God only knows." The Supervisor took off his hat and wiped his bald head with his sleeve. His whole face glistened with sweat. "But now folks, we've got to get back to business. Our country is at war and we've got to change some things. The company plans to keep all of us as safe as possible. You can take my word on that."

"God bless our soldiers and sailors!" Maybelle yelled.

"God bless President Roosevelt!" Cheers went up.

A slim woman in a yellow dress clamored up on a folding chair. She put her hand over her heart and held her head erect. It was Mrs. Sullards, my math teacher from the school. "Oh, say can you see, by the dawn's early light." She sang in a quivery voice that gave me the chills.

Other woman put their hands over their hearts and picked up the song. "What so proudly we hail."

All the older kids in the room joined the choir. "At the twilight's last gleaming."

Mr. Moore pulled off his hat and put it over his heart. "And the rockets' red glare."

One of the men who had come in with Mr. Moore squared his shoulders and snapped off a salute. "The bombs bursting in air."

I had heard our national anthem a zillion times before that day, but I'd never heard that song rendered with more fervor and emotion than I heard it that morning in a crowded, hot social club on the banks of Lake Maracaibo just hours after the Japanese bombed Pearl Harbor.

I joined in the singing that morning with as much spirit as I had in me. My only problem was as the song swelled to its grand crescendo—"o'er the land of the free and the home of the brave"—all my thoughts were with a freckle-faced German girl who took my heart with her when she vanished into the Venezuelan hills.

⟪ 18 ⟫

The next few weeks in the Creole Camp were an odd combination of pretending everything was back to normal and adjusting to a situation that was about as far from normal as you could get.

America went to war with Germany and school resumed. Same lessons, same teachers, but somehow nothing was the same. Nobody cut up in class anymore. Nobody laughed much either. Sonny and his gang were suddenly nice to me. I don't mean they invited me to sit with them at lunch or anything, but the feeling Sonny and I were always about to have a fight disappeared.

Everyone did their homework. Somehow being good students seemed like the patriotic thing to do. Mrs. Sullards had a brother who joined the navy after Pearl Harbor, and about every other day, she would get weepy over the slightest thing and have to leave the room to compose herself. We'd all just go on with our work. Nobody clowned around or threw spitballs. That would have seemed disrespectful.

At school, at home, at the Club everybody talked endlessly about how important oil production was to the war effort. Even the newspapers talked on and on about how the key to winning the war was America's industrial capacity. We had to produce more guns, bombs, planes, trucks, and ships than the Axis. And that was going to take oil. Lots of oil.

Knowing how important oil production was gave everyone a new sense of how important the Creole Camp was. We were a main source of the oil that was needed to win the war.

Even recognizing the importance of the oil they were producing, several of Daddy's best American workers quit and headed home to join the army or the navy. They wanted to be in the middle of the action, not stuck in some oil camp in the middle of nowhere. Even if what they were doing was helping the war effort. They wanted to fight for their country. Consequently Daddy had to rely more and more on the native workers. The Venezuelans seemed to like him and he never let the derricks' production drop.

I overheard Uncle Harry say that Daddy was a genius at teaching the natives how to run the rigs and at getting them to work hard. Of course I knew Uncle Harry was right there at my father's side, and I suspected he played a key role in making a smooth transition to using the natives on the derricks.

One thing that never felt normal was the armed men who constantly patrolled the camp. Everywhere you looked, there was a company man with a shotgun in the crook of his arm or a pistol strapped on his side. Creole Oil even set up an air patrol on the roof of the Club. Employees with binoculars watched the skies every day. It was extra duty but nobody seemed to mind.

The outbreak of war did solve one problem. I sure didn't need to tell anyone about the German's radio in the bathhouse. What good would that do? Talk about closing the barn door after the horses have already run away.

Most of all I missed Hannah. Before the war broke out, even on the days I didn't see her, there was always the hope that I might see her the next day. Or the one after that. But after Pearl Harbor everything changed. She and the other Germans had vanished. Period. My only hope was someday, somehow, Hannah and I would meet again. I clung to that dream like a drowning man holds on to a life raft.

Clutching that faint hope, I went home from school every day, did my chores, threw myself grounders in the backyard, and dreamed about Hannah. Where was she? Was she really hiding in the hills? Had she been picked up by the U-boats? Was she on the way back to Germany? There was no way of knowing. And that made me feel crazy.

Strangely enough, with the outbreak of war, everybody quit talking about who killed Mr. Taggert. I know people still thought about the murder, but the war just seemed to push the killing aside. Folks had more important matters to discuss. Until Mama and Daddy had their big fight.

Even though everything looked normal on the surface, you could bet there was a lot of underlying uneasiness in the camp during those weeks—people were worried about what was happening back in the states and what was happening in Europe and the Pacific, how the war was going and all—and that tension boiled over in our house one night a couple of weeks after Pearl Harbor.

The fight started after I'd gone to bed. But it didn't matter. Our house was built out of cheap plywood and you could hear everything everybody said anywhere in the house even if they were just talking normal. But if someone started yelling, well . . . there weren't many secrets in our house.

After supper that night, Mama listened to the Andrews Sisters and Glenn Miller on the phonograph and read old magazines. She seemed nervous and jittery, jumping up and pacing around the living room, emptying ashtrays that had already been emptied.

Daddy sat back in the kitchen, studying some kind of blueprints, while he sipped Ballantine beer out of the bottle. I did my math homework and read some of *Great Expectations*, this mind-numbing book by Charles Dickens about this drippy little kid and how nobody wanted him. He was so drippy I wouldn't have wanted him either.

So anyway, I finished my chapters and my math problems and even talked to Mama for a few minutes about how stupid the book was. She agreed. *Great Expectations* sounded pretty stupid to her too. Then I told Mama and Daddy good night and went to my room, where I put on my pajamas, got in bed, and read a *Captain America* comic until I got sleepy.

But I never got to sleep.

I don't know what started the fight, but I heard

Mama and Daddy's voices getting louder and louder as I snuggled down under the covers. I tried covering my ears with my pillow but that didn't work very well.

"You don't know what's going to happen!" Mama yelled. "We could get bombed just like Pearl Harbor! This is no place for a family!"

"We're fine, Dixie. And you know it." Daddy struggled to keep his voice calm. "The company says there's nothing to worry about. We'd be in more danger if we lived out in California. That's where the next attack will come. I'd bet a month's pay on it."

"The company! You believe what the company says? After all the lying they've done to you and Harry? What happened to that bonus they promised you? What happened to those drum heads or whatever they were that the company promised you? Tell me that."

"Well, Harry figured out a way to retool the old ones," Daddy said. "And like everybody else nowadays, the company's got better things to think about than last year's bonuses. Be fair now."

"Oh, hell's bells, Ches. You're just a pushover. Just as long as they let you go out on the rigs everyday and do whatever it is you do out there you don't care about anything else. You don't even care if Ricky and I get blown to smithereens."

"Now think about what you're saying here. You know that's not true. I love both of you and I need you here with me."

A long silence followed.

Then I heard my Mama sobbing. "I want to go home! I hate it here! I hate this house! I hate those gossipy broads over at the Club! I want to go home! I want to go back to El Dorado. My God! We're at war. I'm tired of reading newspapers that are almost a week old. I want a radio with Winchell and the soap operas. I want to live. I don't want to just sit around in this godforsaken camp and wait to die. I want to see my friends. My gosh, Ches, I even want to see Erlene."

Erlene was Mama's widowed sister up in Little Rock. She was fat and bossy and Mama was never too fond of Aunt Erlene. I knew Mama was really serious if she missed Aunt Erlene.

"Honey, I know things are tough right now, but they'll get better. Stay with me here and you'll see. The company will take care of us."

All I could hear was Mama crying even louder.

Daddy cleared his throat. "Maybe it would help if you could lay off the booze a little. That might make you feel better."

"Oh, that's great. Just great," Mama sobbed. "You drag me down here and make me live in a shanty that white trash back home wouldn't even look at. You make me live in a Wild West nightmare where someone is murdered and his body's left out where our child can find the corpse, and when I take an occasional drink, you want to take that away from me. Thanks, Chester, you're a swell guy."

"It's more than an occasional drink and you know it." There was a real edge in Daddy's voice.

"Leave me alone!"

"Come on, Sugar. Let's don't fight. The war's put everybody's nerves on edge."

"Take me home!"

"Sweetie—"

"Don't you Sweetie me! Get me out of here! Get me and Ricky home! This is no place for a young boy. For all we know there's still a killer running around loose out there. Everybody seems to have forgotten that. We're all probably going to get murdered in our beds. If the Japanese don't bomb us first. Or the Venezuelans go crazy and carve us up with those horrid knives. Please, Ches. Get me out of here. I mean it."

Silence descended on the living room. I imagined Daddy packing his pipe, twisting and thumping it, getting the tobacco just right, and then lighting the pipe, sucking and blowing until the bowl glowed just the way he liked it. I could smell the fresh smoke all the way back in my bedroom.

"We're not going to be murdered in our beds," Daddy said, the anger gone from his voice. "Dixie, honey, listen. We know who murdered Mr. Taggert. It was one of those German fellows. John Long told me himself. Apparently Taggert accidentally found some kind of radio the German employees were using to talk to submarines up north in the Caribbean. They were probably planning some kind of attack on the oil wells in the lake. The Germans were afraid Taggert would tell about the radio and so . . . well . . . they killed him. But whichever one of 'em did it, he's long gone, so you don't have to fret your pretty head about murders and such anymore."

Even through the thin walls of our house, there was something in Daddy's voice that made me uneasy.

Something that made me think he knew more than he was telling Mama. Something that made me think we still had a lot to worry about.

The anger in the tiny house evaporated and things got quiet. In a little while I heard Mama and Daddy go to bed. I lay on my back and stared out the window at the heavens, wondering if Hannah was somewhere in the hills looking at the same shiny moon.

« 19 »

A couple of days later, Daddy took me back out on the rig with him, still hoping that somehow I would become magically fascinated by cables and pumps and lockings and fittings and engines and oil.

It was a waste of time. He walked me around, explained how everything worked, and told me what everything was. I was glad there wasn't going to be a test afterward.

Uncle Harry was breaking in a new crew of native workers and gave me a friendly wave from the sea level platform. The early morning sun pounded the lake, and Uncle Harry had already stripped down to his tank-top undershirt and tied a red bandanna around his head to keep the sweat out of his eyes.

I tried to make myself invisible, lost in the yelling of the men, the pounding of the pump engines, and the smell of body odor and sweat and grease and oil. Always oil.

Something minor went wrong with some gismo that kept the belts tight on this big wheel. Daddy called me over and attacked the problem with a screwdriver that he used to prop up the little levers at the top of the gismo.

He carefully explained exactly what he was doing with each step. "Now watch this. See. I'm tightening the gistflop so the motoronic will keep the flopmo steady. But you don't want to get it too tight because then your heppotronics won't have room to vibrate. And you can see what that would do."

Not in a million years.

Daddy was in heaven. I think sometimes he hoped some of the machinery on the derrick or even in the house would malfunction so he could grab his tools and jump in and fix whatever was wrong.

I stood behind him and mumbled, "Right. Yeah. Sure. That makes sense." It didn't, but I didn't want to disappoint him.

"Say, I've got an idea," my father said after a while. "I'm going to put you on the job. That's always the best way to learn something."

"On the job? Me?"

"Sure. I was just about to get Darcy and Slim Anderson to switch some rotor cables. They could always use an extra hand. It's easy. You just feed them the cable while they rethread it. How does that sound?"

"Great. Swell." Talk about a liar.

So a few minutes later, I found myself on the top platform feeding thick metal cable from a coil on the deck to Darcy and Slim and a pair of Venezuelan workers while they wrapped it evenly around this giant spindle. Slim, despite his name, was a squat, powerfully built bald guy who kept an unlit cigar clamped between his nicotine-stained teeth. Darcy was a skinny guy with leathery skin.

The cable was heavy, and I really had to work and strain to keep it coming to the spindle.

Darcy and Slim were both nice guys who kept up a constant chatter while they worked. It turned out they both loved baseball and the three of us had a lively discussion about which league was better—the American League with the Yankees or the National League which always seemed to have a lot of good teams but no great ones. I told them I was a big Cardinals fan. They both liked the Yankees. Slim had even once seen Babe Ruth play in Yankee Stadium.

"Well, I tell you fellows one thing," Darcy said. "Your Redbirds are gonna need Slim's lucky rabbit's foot if they're gonna have a shot at the pennant this year." He shook his head. "Yessir, you are one lucky cuss," he said to Slim.

"I was due for a hot streak." Slim beamed, his teeth clinched around his cigar.

Darcy winked at me. "Last couple of nights over in the bachelors' quarters, Slim's been the New York Yankees of the poker table. Ain't that right, Slim?"

"Yeah, I reckon so." Slim tried to look modest, but a little smile in the corners of his mouth gave him away. He signaled for me to feed more cable. "But if I was the Yankees, Harry Kramer was sure enough the Washington Senators of the poker table."

Darcy cracked up laughing. "That's a good one. Yessir. Harry was the Washington Senators of the poker table. He couldn't beat anybody. I've never seen a man lose so much on the turn of the cards."

I probably should have said something in Uncle Harry's defense, but it was easier to laugh along with Darcy and Slim. The Senators were far and away the worst team in baseball and the joke was actually pretty funny.

We kept laughing while they wrapped the cable I fed them around the spindle. In a little while Darcy and Slim started talking about what makes a good hunting dog and the morning flew by.

An hour or so later, one of the Venezuelan workers and I spotted the boats at the same time. We were the only two people left on the top platform. Darcy and Slim had finished wrapping the cable and gone to the deck below to help my father with something else. I was sitting on the giant spindle, catching my breath and enjoying the breeze off the lake.

The Venezuelan worker had helped us wrap the cable. He was a powerfully built man with dark skin and long unwashed hair. He looked off in the distance and saw the same thing I did. He stared out at the water for a couple of minutes, mumbled something in Spanish. Then he crossed himself.

The boats were a long way off, little more than dots moving on the horizon, but they were getting closer, coming from the southern end of the lake, slowly and steadily moving toward the derricks. They were long, sleek canoes, too many to count.

The Venezuelan worker started yelling, pointing at the boats. I didn't have any idea what he was shouting, but I didn't need to know. From the tone of his voice, I knew he was scared to death. Whatever was coming was serious trouble.

Other workers rushed to the railing and looked out at the water, shielding their eyes from the sunlight with their palms.

"Holy moley," one of the American workers whispered.

"Get the shotguns!" Another man yelled. "We got big trouble."

I looked out at the horizon. Slowly I recognized what was heading our way. I stared in disbelief and horror at the one thing everyone in the Creole Camp feared more than anything. The canoes rode low in the water and each boat held five or six Indians, straining at the paddles. Each Indian's face was crisscrossed with black and red paint.

The canoes looked like they were skimming along the surface of the lake. They were getting closer and closer, going faster and faster.

My heart started pounding like crazy. I looked around. We were trapped on the rig. There was no place to go. No place to hide.

Suddenly a loud siren went off. Men were running everywhere. Their faces, masks of fear, told me we were in major trouble. All I could think about was how much I wished I could be somewhere else. What was about to happen was too horrible to think about.

Down on the lower platform, three American workers rushed to the railing, putting shells in their shotguns as fast as they could. Uncle Harry was right behind them, a pistol in each hand. He still had the red bandana across his forehead.

Daddy appeared in one of the walkways below me. He had his fedora tilted back. He also had a pistol in his hand. I had always thought of my father as a peaceful man, but I could tell from the look on his face that he could also be a fighter if the occasion called for it.

A pair of Venezuelan workers came out on the platform where I was glued to the railing, unable to move. Both of them had machetes in their hands. I wanted to cry but couldn't even breathe. The blades shimmered in the sun. Daddy had told me the workers were forbidden to bring weapons onto the derricks, but at the moment I was glad to see their long knives. The men talked to each other in excited Spanish. In the torrent of words, I caught the word "Motilone"—the Indians who had once lived on the shore of the lake and had been driven to the south when the rigs came in.

The first wave of canoes approached the derrick. In each boat two or three of the Indians stood up, produced enormous bows, and loaded them with long arrows. They took aim at the oil rig.

"Get down! Get down!" one of the American workers called from the lower platform. "They dipped them arrowheads in poison. Get down."

The Indians released their arrows at once. A rain of death fell on the rig. The tips of the arrows clanked on the metal floor of the platform. One of the Venezuelan workers screamed. I had ducked back into a tiny overhang, jamming myself against it as hard as I could, my eyes shut tight, afraid to look. When I did look out again the worker was writhing on the deck, an arrow embedded in his calf.

I curled up into a tight ball, pulling my knees deep into my chest. My breath came in shallow gasps. I couldn't stop shaking.

The men on the platform below fired their shotguns. One of the Indians flew out of his canoe and splashed into the lake. The water turned a dark red where he landed.

At the far end of the derrick, one of the Indian canoes glided up to the planking and a pair of Indians jumped onto the rig. A second boat docked right behind them. From my vantage point under the overhang, I saw Uncle Harry sprinting down the walkway toward the invaders. He fired one pistol and then another one on the run. The first Indian's face exploded into a bloody mass. Uncle Harry fired again. The bullet hit the second Indian in the chest, turning him completely around.

A third Indian threw a knife at Uncle Harry. Uncle Harry ducked the missile, dropped to one knee, and shot the invader in the leg. The man tumbled backward into the water.

Behind me, I heard another barrage of arrows clanging on the top platform. One of the workers screamed in pain. I whirled around and saw one of the Americans fall backward with an arrow stuck in his shoulder. Nothing in my life had prepared me for what I was witnessing. This was horror on a level I never dreamed possible. My stomach convulsed and the taste of vomit filled my mouth.

Looking down between the gaps in the metal mesh

walkway, I saw Daddy aim his pistol at one of the canoes. The thing I'll always remember about that moment was that my father had his pipe clutched tight in the side of his mouth. Death danced all around him and Daddy still had his pipe in his mouth. It was the bravest thing I had ever seen. My father, his pipe and his pistol, right up front fighting. Talk about courage.

My dad sighted down the barrel of his pistol and fired. I never saw if his bullet found its mark. I ducked down as more arrows hit the platform.

The whole world had spun out of control. People around me were hurt and bleeding. Grown men were crying. My heart thumped so loud I thought my chest would explode.

On the lower platform, the men with the shotguns opened fire again. This time several Indians tumbled out of the boats and splashed into the murky lake.

Another barrage of arrows rained on the top platform. I huddled under the overhang until they stopped. I was crazy with fear, and the fear made me even crazier. I sprinted out of my hiding place and took the stairs leading down to the lower platform three at a time. I don't know what I thought I was going to do, but running felt better than cringing under the overhang, waiting for the worst to happen.

By the time I got to the end of the platform at the far end of the derrick, another half-dozen Indians poured over the railing. I froze at the bottom of the stairs. One of the Venezuelan workers charged past me, his machete at the ready. He waded into the Indians, swinging the machete with careful strokes. I watched in horror.

The Venezuelan caught one of the Indians across the throat and almost took his head off. In an instant only a thin strand of bone and cartilage held the man's head to his neck. Blood shot into the air like oil gushing from a new well. I looked away.

Uncle Harry emptied both pistols into the Indians who were still up on the railing. The impact of the bullets drove both of them back into the water below.

Off to my left, another pair of Indians swung themselves over the railing and landed on the platform. The first one pulled an arrow from the quiver on his back and strung the arrow into his bow.

"Uncle Harry!" I yelled at the top of my lungs. "Look out! Behind you!"

The Indian let the arrow fly.

Uncle Harry whirled around and dove off to his left. The arrow hit the deck and skidded harmlessly into the corner.

The second Indian pulled a stubby looking pistol from his belt, took aim, and fired at the Venezuelan worker with the machete. The bullet caught the man high on the shoulder. The Venezuelan grabbed his arm and slumped against the railing.

Uncle Harry came up on one knee and fired both his guns at the Indian with the pistol. The Indian's body flew backwards against the rail. His gun clattered on the metal deck.

The other Indian fired another arrow and this one found its mark—in Uncle Harry's right leg, just above the knee. The arrow passed all the way through his flesh and came out on the other side. At first Uncle Harry looked surprised and then his face contorted with pain. He dropped both guns and clutched at the wound.

This couldn't be happening. None of this could be happening. Uncle Harry's face twisted with pain. He clawed at the arrow in his leg. Blood soaked his pants.

The Indian reached back into his quiver. Before he could get another arrow out, a pair of Venezuelan workers tackled him from behind. They started beating him with their fists.

I sprinted across the deck to help Uncle Harry. He was sprawled in the middle of the platform. I knew that was a dangerous place to be, but I couldn't leave Uncle Harry out there. Not Uncle Harry. I grabbed him under the arms and dragged him across the deck. Uncle Harry was a big man. I grunted and strained and pulled and put all my strength into getting him across the platform to the shelter of the stairwell. Just as we made it to the overhang, another broadside of arrows cascaded on the platform and plinked on the metal floor where Uncle Harry had been.

I was gasping for air. I looked down at Uncle Harry. In the movies or the comics, the Uncle Harry character would give me a wink or a smile or the okay sign. But this was the real thing and Uncle Harry just grimaced in pain. Spittle ran down his chin.

I left him for a second and dashed back across the platform to retrieve his guns. When I got back, I tried to give the weapons to him, but he was soaked in sweat and his face was turning gray. He barely seemed to know who I was or what was going on.

Poison! Someone had yelled that the Indians put poison on their arrows.

I had done a good bit of pistol shooting back in El Dorado. Daddy loved guns. He knew everything in the world about them. He used to take me down to the bayous, and we'd put tin cans and beer bottles on stumps and take target practice at them. So I was comfortable with a gun in my hand.

I checked the chamber of one of Uncle Harry's .38s, made sure it held a bullet, and popped it shut. I cocked the hammer. The gun was ready. Uncle Harry let out a low moan. I crouched down and put my mouth close to his ear. "You're gonna be okay, Uncle Harry," I whispered, the words tumbling out of my mouth, tripping all over each other. "Daddy'll be here in a minute. We'll get you to the hospital. Hang on. Everything's gonna be all right."

The battle raged out on both main platforms. Gunfire echoed off the steel girders, and arrows clanged on the deck. The weird thing was the engines kept going and the big pumps never stopped during the fight.

And then the attack ended as suddenly as it had started. I guess the Indians must have realized they weren't going to be able to capture the derrick and figured they had lost enough men. They turned their canoes around and headed back across the lake.

The platforms were littered with bodies. Indians, Venezuelans, Americans. Hurt, dead, bleeding. The smell of gunpowder mingled with the sharp smell of grease, oil, and machinery.

Daddy found Uncle Harry and me under the

overhang. Uncle Harry had lost consciousness. His mouth hung open, but his breathing was steady. All around us, workers scrambled back and forth, pouring out a steady stream of rapid Spanish.

My father bent down and checked Uncle Harry's damaged leg. The look on Daddy's face told me the wound was serious. "Don't worry son," Daddy said to me. "Harry's as tough a man as you'll ever meet. He'll be all right. We'll get him and the other wounded men back to the camp. You go with them. I want you off the rig. I should never have brought you out here. I'll stay here with the others. We'll guard the rig until the company can send reinforcements. You did good, Rick. Looks like you took care of Harry. I'm proud of you."

A Venezuelan worker ran up to Daddy with a pistol one of the Indians had used. He handed the gun to Daddy and talked in rapid-fire Spanish. Daddy examined the gun and let out a long sigh.

"It's a German made Luger," he said, shaking his head. "I don't know where they got a weapon like this one, but I can guess."

He patted Uncle Harry's head, which was slumped over on the deck. "A German made pistol, Harry. I guess the war has reached our shores, old friend. And we are now officially deep in the dog's business."

« 20 »

I had been a part of one of the first battles of the war. What a way to start my teen years! The Germans had armed the Indians, and they had tried to destroy an oil-producing rig that was important to the war effort. And I had been there. The history books would never mention the fighting on Lake Maracaibo that day. They saved the ink for the regular army and the navy and the marines. But I always would know I had been a part of history.

After the skirmish on the lake, I couldn't concentrate on my schoolwork. Diagraming sentences and doing math problems didn't seem to be important. I couldn't even make it all the way through a comic book without my mind jumping to something else. It was really weird.

But I still dreamed about Hannah. Still thought about her all the time. Still promised myself I'd find her someday. But I'd been in the war. I'd seen people shot and hurt. It wasn't like the battles in the comic books. In real life people cried and moaned and screamed when they were injured. Fighting wasn't fun at all. War wasn't heroic.

"There's no question about it," Daddy said at the breakfast table a week or so after the raid. "The Germans are arming the Motilones. My guess is the German navy wants to destroy the derricks one way or the other. They know how valuable the oil we produce here is to the Allied cause."

Mama and Daddy and I were sitting around the table, eating breakfast. The morning sun made its first appearance of the day and little motes floated every which way in the sunlight.

"So you think the Indians will try again?" Mama sipped a cup of coffee. She seemed more interested in the coffee than the food. She looked worried and haggard like she had been sick and hadn't had enough sleep. She just pushed her eggs around on her plate and then took another sip of coffee.

"I'm sure they will. Don't know when, but it's just a matter of time." Daddy's glance wandered out the window at the palm tree in our backyard. I had noticed he had been doing that a lot since the attack on the rig—talking about something and then losing his train of thought and staring out a window or losing himself in his pipe ritual. I guess the battle on the lake had messed up his concentration just like it had mine.

Mama rubbed her eyes with the back of her hand. Just talking seemed to take a lot out of her. "You think some of the Germans that worked here and lived over in the compound are helping to arm the Indians? That would be just like them, wouldn't it? Like dogs biting the hand that fed 'em."

I looked down at the gooey eggs on my plate. I had

been thinking the same thing, but was too chicken to say anything. Werner and Fritz. Maybe even Dr. Oudt. And Hannah? Was she fixing sandwiches or something for the Germans who went off to arm the Indians? Maybe she was helping to take the guns to the Motilones. Cheering them on, saying something like, "Here. Take a gun and go shoot Ricky. Or shoot Ricky's father. Or put an arrow through Uncle Harry's leg."

The more I thought about it, the more I realized Hannah had never actually told me what she thought of Hitler and the Nazis. She never said something like "Hitler is the biggest jerk in the history of mankind." But she had also never said something like "ole Adolph is the greatest thing since sliced bread." She had just never said, one way or the other. I wasn't sure what I thought about that but thinking about it sure unleashed my imagination like a wild mustang on the plains. And those thoughts made me really, really sad.

"It almost has to be the Germans from the compound," Daddy said, mopping up the last of his eggs with a piece of toast. "They'd know which rigs to hit first. How to dismantle the operations. I'm sure the company Germans are in on it. Anything and everything for the Fatherland. But I'm also guessing they're being helped by some military people. Probably snuck in here on a U-boat. Maybe German sailors."

Mama pushed away her half-eaten breakfast and lit a cigarette. The blue smoke curled toward the ceiling. "Harry told me a couple of the Venezuelans swear they saw white men in the canoes that day." She plucked some loose tobacco off her lip.

"I wouldn't argue with that. I didn't see 'em myself, there was an awful lot happening at once, huh, Ricky?"

"Yessir. I don't reckon I'll ever forget it."

Mama snorted. "Both of you are just lucky to be alive. That's all I can say. When I think about what might have happened to both of you I just feel sick all over." She took another drag on her cigarette and then smiled at us. "My two brave men," she said and then teared up.

"There's rumors up at the office we may get some American marines down here to help us guard the rigs," Daddy said. "Washington knows what we're up against. And Lord knows we sure could use the help. We've got plenty of guns, but we're running low on ammunition. But the company is doing everything they can."

Mama snorted again. "What about getting us out of here? Is the company saying anything about that? Or are they too cheap to spend the money? I guess they just want to leave women and children down here to suffer at the hands of the savages. I reckon it would be cheaper to send us all back to the states in pine boxes."

Daddy winced. "Don't talk that way Dixie. I'm sure the company will get all of you back home just as soon as they can. As a matter of fact, I spent most of yesterday morning over at the admin building. I begged and pleaded with Moore to get all the women and children back to the states as soon as possible."

Mama raised her eyebrows.

"Lord knows I'd miss you and Ricky something

fierce, but the camp is no place for the two of you right now. Moore agreed with me. But there's so much going on right now."

Mama angrily tapped her ash into the black plastic ashtray on the table. "In the meantime we'll just go on living in the House of Fear, thinking every day the Germans or the Indians or whoever is gonna strike when we least expect it."

"Honey, please."

Mama fixed Daddy with an angry stare. Neither one of them said a word for the longest time. I sopped up the egg goo on my plate with a piece of toast, popped it in my mouth, and chewed on it quietly, keeping my eyes on my plate. I felt like I was sitting on the rim of a volcano that was about to explode.

Then Mama crushed out her smoke in the ashtray. "You're right," she said without much conviction. "Complaining is not gonna help things any. I'm sorry." She let out a long sigh through her nose. "I reckon I better fix Harry a plate of eggs and make him some more coffee. His appetite seemed a mite better yesterday." She stood up and pushed back her chair. She tried to smile at Daddy and me again, but her lips weren't really into it.

Uncle Harry was asleep in my room. After the attack on the oil derrick, the doctor had removed the arrow, but my father said it was a painful procedure and Uncle Harry ran a real risk of infection that might cost him his leg. A fever had set in and for a day or so Uncle Harry was delirious.

Mama and Daddy and I had visited him every day

in the hospital. The company infirmary had been crowded every time we went. Several company employees had been hurt or wounded in the attack on the oil well and a couple of them had to be in beds out in the hallway. I saw the doctor who had fixed up Daddy's hand scurrying around, reading charts tied to the ends of the beds and giving orders to a couple of nurses. He still had a cigarette dangling from the corner of his mouth.

Uncle Harry's room was at the end of the corridor. He was propped up in bed with his wounded leg resting on a stack of pillows. The leg was wrapped in a thick white bandage but blood had seeped through the gauze. The room smelled like rotting leaves in late autumn.

Uncle Harry's eyes were open, but they were glassy looking. Mama said he was on a lot of painkillers. Whenever he got restless, Mama would hold his hand, and Daddy would sit on the side of the bed while I stood off in the corner. Then we'd just listen to Uncle Harry babble about a bunch of nothing.

Mama hadn't been able to stand seeing him all alone in the hospital, so when he had started feeling better, she had said he sure couldn't go back to the bachelor barracks. She'd had Daddy move Uncle Harry into my room where she could look after him. Mama had been a nurse before she met Daddy, and I think having somebody to nurse helped take her mind off all her troubles.

I slept on the living room sofa and was glad to do it. Uncle Harry was a real hero. Wounded in battle. It was an honor to sleep on the sofa so he could be more comfortable. But I couldn't fight off a growing sense of dread and sadness. What if Uncle Harry lost this leg? He'd never done anything but work on the rigs. What if he couldn't do that anymore? What if he changed? What if he wasn't funny and full of life anymore? What if he wasn't Uncle Harry anymore?

Sometimes, in the afternoons, I'd go in my room and visit with Uncle Harry for a few minutes. He still liked to tell stories about the old wildcatting days back in Texas, when he and Daddy were young and raising hell. I laughed too loud and kidded around too much. I didn't want Uncle Harry to change. I didn't quite believe all of the stories but as long as he kept telling them, he was still Uncle Harry.

Daddy had also gone over to the bachelor barracks and brought Uncle Harry's motorbike over to our house where it'd be safe and would remind Uncle Harry of another reason to get better. He'd parked the bike out on the screened-in back porch so the Harley wouldn't rust in the rain. When Uncle Harry got a little better, I planned to ask him if I could ride the bike around the camp. Even with Hannah gone, I still wanted to ride the Harley. I had convinced myself that I could figure out all the confusing gears, the throttle, the starter, and stuff if I had a chance.

I just knew I could do it. It couldn't be that hard. Could it?

Witnessing the bloody battle on the oil rig plus losing Hannah forever had left me with the major mopes. It was all I could do to drag myself out of bed every morning. I sat around in my pajamas until Mama made me get dressed. Every meal tasted like cardboard. All I could think about was Hannah being somewhere up in the hills with that craphead Fritz. Who knew what could happen in the tropical moonlight? Two people torn from their moorings. Thrown together by fate. Geez.

On top of those thoughts taunting me, Mama had turned into a drill sergeant. She was always barking orders at me, making up stupid chores like alphabetizing the canned goods or beating the rugs on the clothesline out back to get rid of the dust. She couldn't sit still. After bridge at the Club every day, she slurred her words and walked into the furniture.

On the weekends I walked over to the deserted baseball field where I sat in the bleachers by myself and thought about Hannah and how much I missed her.

One Saturday afternoon I was sitting on the top row of the bleachers, my chin resting in my hands, my mind drifting, when I saw two figures come out of the jungle beyond left field.

The day felt cool and thick gray clouds filled the sky. Rain was coming.

The figures shuffled along, moving across the outfield, heading toward the bleachers. They were both tall and hatless. One of them wore canvas pants and a tank-top undershirt despite the late afternoon chill. The other figure had on brown pants and a blue shirt. When they reached the pitcher's mound, I recognized the guy in the tank top. It was Romulo, the Venezuelan kid with the amazing curve ball. I didn't know the other guy.

When they reached home plate, Romulo waved. I waved back.

They stopped at the bottom of the bleachers and gazed around the baseball field. They looked nervous. I couldn't blame them. The natives were not supposed to be in our camp. Satisfied we were alone, they looked up at me.

"Chew are Ricky Parker?" the guy in the blue shirt called up to me. He was about Romulo's age and his accent was thick. "We have been searching for chew."

"You been looking for me?"

"Si."

"What for?"

"May we come up?"

I shrugged. "Sure."

Romulo and his friend climbed the bleachers and sat down in front of me. Romulo introduced me to the guy in the blue shirt. The guy's name sounded like "GoMo."

"I am from a village on the north end of the lake,"

GoMo said. "Romulo is my cousin."

I wasn't sure what I was supposed to do with that information.

Romulo smiled at me and made the sign of a breaking ball with his hand. I grinned back at him and placed two fingers on my chest. He laughed.

"I learn a little English from my mother," GoMo said. "She once work in Maracaibo."

"You sound great," I said.

"I try to teach Romulo, but is no easy."

I could tell he was kidding his cousin.

"Fassbull," Romulo said.

"Right." I put one finger on my chest.

"I have a letter," GoMo said.

"A letter?"

"Si."

I had no idea what the guy was talking about.

"Lass week," GoMo went on. "Many peoples pass through my village. Gringos who work the land wells. Some with their families. They head for the hills to the south.

The Germans!

"I am watching them as they pass through the square. They stop for food and drink at my uncle's bar. They appear weary. A girl crosses the square and speaks to me in the English. She is happy I understand. We make a deal for the business. She gives me many pesos if I bring a letter to the Creole Camp and give it to Ricky Parker. Is you? I not know anyone here but Romulo. He say he know Ricky Parker. Is baseball catcher. He help me find you."

I couldn't breathe. My insides churned like a whirlwind had attacked my gut. I didn't need to ask what the girl looked like.

"I will go to America someday. Make many deals of business. Make much money." GoMo beamed.

Romulo shot him an elbow in the ribs.

"Ah, yes. The letter. Is here." GoMo dug around in the back pocket of his pants and produced a crumbled cream-colored envelope. Some of the ink on the address had smudged. I could still make out my name and the words "Creole Camp."

"I give it to Ricky Parker," GoMo said, handing me the envelope. "Is what I promised the senorita." He beamed with pride.

"Thank you." The words came out in a weak whisper. I held the letter like a newborn puppy.

Romulo tugged on his cousin's arm.

"We must go now, Ricky Parker. Is not safe for us here. Is time of war," GoMo said.

I nodded.

"Is good-bye, Ricky Parker. You are a fine catcher," Romulo said.

"And you are a hell of a pitcher," I said. "I owe you." I indicated the letter.

Rumulo grinned.

He and his cousin scrambled down the bleachers and hit the baseball field at a dead run. In a matter of seconds they disappeared back into the jungle beyond left field.

I sat and looked at the unopened letter. The sun was vanishing over the compound in the distance and my jacket wasn't doing much of a job of holding back the evening chill. I didn't care. I could have been at the North Pole and it wouldn't have mattered. My body tingled and my breathing was loud and labored.

I ran my thumb under the envelope's seal and pulled out three pages covered with loopy, feminine handwriting. For a minute I thought about not reading the letter. Then I would never know and that might be better than the truth. But I had to know. One way or the other.

So I leaned back against the bleacher seats behind me, snapped open the letter and started reading.

> *Dearest Ricky:*
>
> *I can only hope and pray that this letter reaches you. The mail is not so reliable in Venezuela so I will try to find another way to get it to you. And it is wartime also and I know it would be a miracle if my letter made it back to the Creole Camp and found you. But I had to write it anyway.*
>
> *I fear the winds of war have driven us apart and the thought of never seeing you again fills me with a sadness I never knew was possible. You are in my thoughts every minute of every day. That day at my house, in the pantry and at the swimming pool you touched something so deep in me, I can only call it my soul.*

Life has been so hard these last few weeks that only my thoughts of you and my dream that someday we will see each other again are the only things that make life worthwhile.

You will never know the shock I felt that Sunday morning we were awakened before the rising of the sun. There was much confusion and anger and before we knew what was happening my whole family was fleeing through the jungle. We were only allowed to carry one small suitcase and I cried again and again when I thought of my beautiful things I had to leave back in the camp—my ballerina figurines, my cherry wood jewelry box, even my little stuffed dog I've had since I was a tiny girl in Heidelberg.

Our journey took two entire days. On the second day, we left the jungle and climbed into the hills. Beautiful vistas of the lake marked our every step, but there was no time to stop and admire the scenery.

We finally arrived at a campsite in the middle of a plateau. The site had crude huts and fire pits. Werner and Fritz laughed at my amazement. They said the young men who went off to work the land rigs had more to do than pull oil out of the ground for the enemies of the Fatherland. Fritz said all of the men had known war with the Americans was coming, and they had prepared for the future.

My poor father did not know. He is shattered by all that has happened. Each day he sits alone on a log on the edge of the campsite, staring at the lake in the distance, shaking his head and muttering about the folly of mankind.

Sometimes he speaks of strange things that begin happening in the Creole compound the minute the wave of Americans that brought you to me arrived. When I ask him of what he speaks, he mumbles something about thieves and men of no character and then he changes the subject. I fear all of this has been too much for dear papa. He refuses to eat or even to wash. He never dreamed affairs would reach this state.

Each day I help my mother with little Hans, help her with the cooking and all the things that make life in the wilderness tolerable. At night I look at the stars and think of you and our beautiful moments together. No matter what happens in the future we will always remember the moments of magic that belong to only you and me.

Last night Fritz told us what is to come. The younger men are going to stay in the hills until they are contacted by our navy. After that he doesn't know what will happen. At least he says he doesn't.

Hans, my mother and all the other women, including me are to rendezvous with a U-boat in the northern waters that will take us to a ship and we are all to return to the Fatherland.

Oh, Ricky, Ricky, we will never see each other again. We will never know what might have been for you and I. I'm crying my heart out as I write this. The feelings I have for you are the most powerful I have ever known. They are stronger than the hatred that drives our two countries apart. For countries to go to war is wrong. The armies fight over land and power and foolish things. And they destroy beautiful things like love.

Even though we will never see each other again, my feelings for you will never die. Even if I survive the return to Deutschland and the coming war, my love for you will last forever and forever. You will always be the object of my heart's affection.

Ricky, if you ever get to the Angel Falls, no matter when or how old you are, promise me that when you see the beauty of the magnificent waterfall for the first time, promise me that your first thought will be of me. And I will promise you that my first thought will be of you.

I must close this letter now and seal it with my heart and my tears. Even though the world has gone mad, somehow, some way the power of my love will guide this letter to you.

Be always safe my love and always remember your Hannah.

Yours until the rivers all run dry,
Hannah

≪ 22 ≫

I read Hannah's letter over and over. Again and again. Every day. I read it like the sacred text of a lost civilization. For its knowledge and wisdom and insight. Mostly I read the letter for love.

A couple of weeks after GoMo gave me the letter, rumors of another Indian attack got thicker than the summertime mosquitoes back in El Dorado. Everybody talked about it in the Club and in the general store and in the bachelor barracks. They talked about it anytime and anywhere company people got together.

The time had come to circle the wagons. Everyone had rifles and shotguns by the kitchen door. Every man in the Creole Camp slept with a pistol under his pillow. I imagined things weren't too different over in Europe where the Nazis seemed to be running wild. Welcome to Fear City.

But we never talked about fear in our house. Daddy wouldn't allow it. He headed out to the rigs every morning before the sun came up and returned tired and dirty every evening after dark. He and Uncle Harry drank beer and played gin rummy in my room every night. They laughed and joked like they always had, Uncle Harry ever the rebel, my father ever walking the straight and narrow path. Friends to the end.

And that was life in the camp on Lake Maracaibo. Like the phony war in Europe after the Germans invaded Poland, when everyone was at war, but no one was fighting and a strange and eerie stillness permeated the world.

The phony war in Europe ended abruptly when the Nazis unleashed the awful fury of their evil war machine on the innocent people of Denmark, Norway, and then Belgium, Holland, and France. And the phony war on Lake Maracaibo ended when the Motilone Indians launched their long-awaited second attack on the camp. Only this time they had lots of help.

The first wave of the attack struck in the middle of a peaceful afternoon. It was a quiet Sunday. Just like Pearl Harbor.

Daddy and Mama and I were having lunch on the roof of the Club. Cool breezes blew across the roof, which felt like an escape to the beach. The Club staff had set up picnic tables in the shade of giant beach umbrellas and put out a buffet of cold cuts, potato salad, baked beans, and homemade peach ice cream. A bartender sold drinks from a makeshift bar in the corner of the roof. Someone had hung red, white, and blue bunting along the chest-high wall that enclosed the roof of the club.

I was sipping a Coca-Cola, sitting at one of the picnic tables with Sonny and Will Cole. With the outbreak of the war, we had called a truce and that Sunday we were shooting the breeze about my favorite subject—the Cardinals' chances for the upcoming season.

Our parents were having a drink together a couple of tables over. Daddy looked uncomfortable in a white shirt and tie, but Mama enjoyed the chance to put on her nice Sunday print dress with the blue flowers all over it and get out and talk to other people.

Other adults sat in groups of fours and sixes at the other picnic tables or stood around in clusters talking and sipping drinks and having a fine time.

Until, they heard the gunfire.

Everybody froze. The shots were close. And there were lots of them. Daddy and Mr. Cole jumped up from their picnic table and rushed to the wall.

Sonny and Will and I were right behind them. The back wall faced the east. We could look past the bachelor barracks and the giant pipes and see the beginning of the dense jungle beyond.

Suddenly the jungle came alive. Hundreds of Indians rushed out of the foliage and sprinted across the fields toward the pipes. Most of the Indians had bows and quivers of arrows on their backs and knives in their hands. Some of the ones in the front of the charge had pistols. Their faces were streaked with red-and-black war paint.

Off to our left, the next wave of attackers poured through the pipes and exploded onto the road. These attackers wore white uniforms and white caps with blue bands.

"German sailors!" Sonny's father said. "The Nazis have joined forces with the Motilones. We're in for it now!"

A half-dozen Creole workers and another half-dozen company security men, armed with shotguns and rifles, ran past the bachelor barracks. They fired on the charging Indians. Gun barrels appeared out of the barracks' upper story windows and fired volley after volley at the Indians. The shots dropped several of the attackers.

Behind us, the door to the lower floor flew open and John Long burst onto the roof. He wore crossed bandolier bullet belts across his chest and held a rifle in his hand. "Everybody listen!" He tried to sound calm, but his voice quivered. "I've got all our guns and ammo. We'll have to make a stand here at the Club. It's our only hope."

Several men rushed for the door to get downstairs and get the guns. Someone yelled, "Remember the Alamo!"

A chubby woman standing near me dropped her drink, the glass shattered on the rooftop. She threw her hands over her mouth and burst into sobs. Another woman draped a comforting arm around the chubby woman's shoulder and hugged her tight.

I put my hands on the top of the wall and leaned out to see what was going on. My head reeled and my heart tried to leap right out of my chest. I pressed my shaking hands tight against the wall to steady them.

In the distance, a few yards from the first of the giant pipes, I spotted a pair of Germans in dark trousers and white civilian shirts. They were leading about half a dozen Indians armed with pistols. The man in front stopped and pointed off to his left in the direction of the bachelor's barracks. He was hatless and his whitish-blond hair stood out in sharp contrast to his dark-haired followers.

Fritz!

The second man had on a crumpled fedora, but they were too far away for me to tell if it was Werner. I didn't really want to know. I didn't really want to know if Hannah's brother was out there directing a band of armed Indians intent on killing all of us.

It felt strange to know the names of the attackers. In the comics the enemy was always just the bad guy, a group of nameless, unrecognizable soldiers or spacemen or thugs. Killing them seemed much easier than killing someone whose name you knew. Even if he was a craphead like Fritz.

I felt a hand on my shoulder and jumped.

"Easy, Son," Daddy said, his teeth clinched tight around his pipe stem. "Calm down. Everything's gonna be all right."

Oh, yeah, sure. Everything was just gonna be hunky-dory. We're standing on a roof watching wild Indians and murderous Germans fan out through our camp looking for Americans to slaughter. Right, yeah. Everything's jake, Dad.

"We've got a lot of firepower on our side," Daddy said, his voice calm. "And a lot of men who know how to shoot. And the Venezuelans will probably fight on our side. Remember how we drove the Indians back when we were out on the rig? We'll be all right."

"Yessir."

"Now, here's what I need you to do." Daddy took a deep breath. "Stay with your mother no matter what. You understand me?"

"Yessir, but . . . where will you be?"

He gave me a look that was pure steel. "Me and some of the fellows from here are going to round up the loyal native workers and head out to the rigs.

"But Daddy—"

"Look, Son, this assault is probably just a diversion. It's the derricks they want. I'm betting they'll come at the rigs from the south with dynamite."

"You think they want to blow up the rigs?" I could barely get the words out of my suddenly parched throat.

Let 'em blow the rigs, I wanted to scream. Stay here with me and Mama. We'll be safe if you're here. Forget the stupid oil derricks just this once. Stay here with us, Daddy, please.

"Yessir. I'll . . . I'll look after Mama." I squared my shoulders trying to look as manly as possible despite what I felt inside.

"I know I can count on you, Son."

Daddy nodded and walked over to Mama, who was standing next to the wall. He put his arms around her. She tilted her head and Daddy kissed her hard and long like they do in the movies.

And my father was gone. Just like that. Gone to put his life on the line for an oil derrick.

A couple of minutes later the rooftop exploded into a beehive of activity. John Long barked orders and a group of men stacked sandbags on the top of the wall, all around the roof. The attackers weren't close enough to shoot at, but several men with rifles took up posts along our newly created fortress. Everyone moved with a sense of purpose. Mama and I stood together by the door to the downstairs, looking for something we could do to help.

The sun was broiling. My white Sunday shirt was soaked. My damp hair clung to my forehead and my eyes stung with salty sweat.

"Oh, my god, Ricky." Mama started wringing her hands. "Harry! What are we going to do? He's back at the house. He can't walk on that leg. They'll kill him if they find him." Her eyes filled with tears. "We can't leave him to die like that."

She was right. But what could we do about it? "Mama, we can't go back there." I tried to sound calm. Like my dad. "Daddy said I needed to stay with you. There's nothing we can do for Uncle Harry. How would we bring him back here? He can't walk and we can't carry him."

"We can't leave him. That's all there is to it." Mama grabbed my arm and dragged me to the corner of the wall. She pointed out over the expanse of fields and pipes that led to the edge of the jungle. "Look over there. See? The Indians are following that German man, the blond-headed one. They're headed toward the administration building. Away from our house. If I can get one of the men to go with me, we could get Harry back here. We can't leave him alone in the house. He's helpless."

"Daddy told me to stay with you."

"No, no, honey. You stay here. You'll be safe as long as you stay at the Club. I'll be back as soon as I can."

But things didn't work out that way.

Mama couldn't talk any of the men on the roof into going with her. They all said going back to our house was too risky.

Finally, Mr. Long said there was no way in the world he would let Mama out of the Club. He said Daddy would kill him if he did that.

Mama cried. She pleaded her case, but to no avail. She snapped at Mr. Long, but he didn't change his mind.

Mr. Long told Mama everything would be okay, and then he went back to organizing the defenses on the rooftop.

Mama stood there in the middle of the roof, tears streaming down her cheeks. Other people rushed around her, piling up sandbags, moving furniture, and handing out guns, getting ready for a final attack on the Club.

I put my arm around Mama's shoulder. It hurt to see her cry.

And that's when I got my big brainstorm.

≪ 23 ≫

Sometimes, if you read too many comic books, the line between Captain Marvel and Real Life gets fuzzy. My plan had a few minor flaws, like the fact that I might get killed, but in my comic-book soaked brain, my plan couldn't fail. There was no way.

So I ignored my father's injunction to stay with my mother. And I ignored Mr. Long's contention that we would all be safe if we stayed in the Club. I had a plan and I wasn't about to let any of that dribble stand in my way. Nothing stops Captain Marvel. Or Ricky Parker.

While Mamma searched for someone else to help her, I abandoned my post at the sandbags, went downstairs, snuck into the storage room behind the kitchen, crawled out the window, and started running down the road toward our house in the American compound.

Nobody saw me. Nobody called "Stop! Come back!" or "Use your common sense!" or anything like that, so I just sprinted down the road.

The world outside the Club had been turned upside down. Flames and smoke poured out of the administration building. Gunshots echoed everywhere.

In the distance, flames from the houses of the abandoned British compound licked at the afternoon sky.

But our neighborhood appeared to be deserted. The only sounds were my sneakers pounding on the dirt road and the echoes of gunfire and yelling off in the distance.

I was panting and gasping for air by the time I got to our house. I slowed down and looked around for any signs of the Motilones or the Germans, but didn't see any. Mama must have been right. They were more interested in the buildings surrounding the middle of the camp. The heart and soul of the Creole operation. Plus, Daddy was also probably right: what they really wanted was to destroy the oil rigs.

I circled around our house to the back door and let myself into the silent kitchen. The smell of the morning's fried bacon and cigarette and pipe smoke hung in the kitchen. Light from the afternoon sun swirled from the window above the sink all the way to the breakfast table as it had every day before.

"Uncle Harry! It's Ricky! Are you all right?" I passed through the kitchen and sprinted down the narrow hallway. I opened the door to my bedroom. "Uncle Harry, I—"

Uncle Harry sat propped up on my bed, my cowboy and Indian bedspread pulled up all the way to his chin. His pistol was leveled at the doorway. "Good God, son. You scared me to death. I almost shot you. What's going on out there? I've been hearing shooting for the last hour or so. I tried to get to the living room to take a peek outside, but this leg hurts like the devil if I put any weight on it. Quick, tell me what's happening out there."

I told him about the Indians and the German sailors and the attack on the camp.

"Well, I reckon we're in for it now." Uncle Harry's face was a strange gray color, and he struggled to get his breath. "I think your dad was right on the money. The Germans want to destroy the derricks. Cut off the flow of oil to the allies. Chester'll hold 'em off though. Your daddy's a tough old bird underneath all that pipe puffing and talking the company line."

Uncle Harry kept gesturing with the barrel of his gun. I suspected he had been scared laying there in the bed, hearing the gunshots, and not knowing what was going on outside.

I opened my mouth to tell him about my great plan for us to escape back to the Club, when the first arrow slammed through the bedroom window, shattering the glass and lodging in my little wooden dresser across the room. The arrow kept quivering after it stuck in the wood.

"Geez!" Uncle Harry swung his good leg over the side of the bed and used his hands to get the injured leg to dangle off the edge. He wore an old pair of khaki pants with one leg cut out. The place where the arrow had gone through his thigh was wrapped in a thick gauze bandage. The bandage was heavily stained with a reddish-yellow ooze seeping from the wound. I could smell the infected injury from the doorway.

Cold panic seized my gut. Uncle Harry was in a

bad way. He wasn't going to be much help. Getting him out of the house would be up to me.

"Help me up!" Uncle Harry barked.

I hustled over to the bed, and he pulled himself into a standing position, using my shoulder as a crutch. "Get me over to the window!"

Uncle Harry held his bad leg out at a strange angle and hopped on his good leg until we got to the shattered bedroom window. Balancing himself on one foot, he peered out of the corner of the window. Then he twisted around quickly and blindly fired two shots.

I realized the Indians had probably seen me come into the house and figured out someone else was inside.

"Don't be scared," Uncle Harry said. "We're not what they're after. They're just trying to frighten us. Doing a darn good job of it, I might add." He tried one of those winks and smiles that Errol Flynn and Clark Cable always flashed in the movies when they were in danger. Somehow it didn't work. His lips were so tight, they didn't curl into a full smile. It was more like a grimace. He was terrified. Errol Flynn and Clark Gable were just playing.

A couple of dull thuds pounded against the side of the house. More arrows.

Uncle Harry wheeled around on his good leg and fired another shot out the window. He wasn't aiming the gun, he was just shooting to let them know we were armed.

Suddenly the sound of glass shattering came from the living room.

"Uh-oh. Get me in there, pronto." Uncle Harry

started hopping toward the front of the house on his good leg. He lost his balance. I caught him and acted as a crutch, guiding him into the living room.

Four arrows were stuck in the sofa. From across the room, Uncle Harry fired two more shots out the picture window. "Bottom drawer of the hutch," he gasped. "Your daddy keeps his ammo down there. Grab all the bullets you can. I need to reload."

For a moment, I couldn't imagine leaving Harry and going anywhere. I stood hanging onto him.

"Hustle up, son."

I propped Uncle Harry against the easy chair and found four boxes of bullets in the drawer. I pulled out the bullets and stuffed them in my pants pockets. Then I handed two boxes to Uncle Harry, and he quickly reloaded the pistol and fired three more shots out the window.

A barrage of dull thuds pounded on the side of the house.

"Get me over there," Uncle Harry growled, indicating the side of the window. "Then I can see what's happening."

We did our hop-walk-dance across the living room to the sound of the arrows raining on the side of the house.

Uncle Harry eased himself down to his knees and peeked over the window ledge. Then he fired three more shots at the front yard. "Four of 'em," he said, "Looks like two Indians and a pair of German sailors." He wiped the sweat off his forehead with the back of his hand. "Not too bad. We can hold 'em off. We got plenty of ammo." He pulled his red bandana out of his hip pocket, twirled it into a narrow strip, and tied it around his forehead.

An arrow whistled through the shattered window and lodged in the floor, the feathers quivering.

I jumped and let out a frightened, "Ahh." I walked around the arrow like it was a rattlesnake. Suddenly, I picked up a scent that reminded me of the oily odor on the rig and said, "What's that smell?"

"Walking oil." Uncle Harry peeked over the ledge again. "The Germans are gonna try to burn us out."

"What's walking oil?" I asked, but wasn't sure I wanted to hear the answer.

"A mixture of gunpowder and crude oil." Uncle Harry's breathing was tortured from fear and exertion. "One of them is trailing it around the house. He's about halfway done. Then they'll run it up as close to the house as they can."

"Then what?"

"Then they'll ignite it and torch the house."

My stomach did a bunch of flip-flops. I thought of all my stuff back in my bedroom. The thought of losing all that stuff filled me with sadness. It was only stuff, but, geez. It was _my stuff. My eyes filled up with tears and I felt like a big baby.

Uncle Harry furiously gnawed on his lower lip. "We gotta get outta here, pronto. Once they light the powder, it'll blow in just a minute or so. Damn. I can't walk on this leg. We'd be sitting targets if you have to help me out of the house." He looked back over the windowsill and fired a couple of shots. "The Indian with the powder is already around to the side of the house."

I pressed my back against the wall and sank down on the floor, determined not to cry. My whole body quaked uncontrollably. Tears came anyway.

More thuds thumped against the front of the house. Uncle Harry cringed.

My mind raced, desperately searching for a way out. There wasn't one.

"We've got to think of something quick," Uncle Harry said.

I pounded the side of my head with my fists. There had to be a way. There had to be something we could do.

Uncle Harry's eyes grew wide with fear.

"I . . . I have an idea." My voice shook as I fought back the tears.

"I'm open to suggestions. Just make it quick."

"I had the idea when I came over here. I thought it would be a way to get you back to the Club with your bad leg. I still think it might work."

"Whatever it is, it's better than what I got, which is nothing. Let's hear it."

I told Uncle Harry my idea. He grabbed my shoulder and gave it a hard squeeze. "Your daddy's not the only one in your family with a head on his shoulders. That's our way out. Get going. I'll take care of my end."

I pushed myself off the floor and sprinted across the living room. Just as I reached the kitchen door, there was a loud whoosh and the whole house shook from an explosion. The Indians had ignited the walking oil. Every window in the house filled with bright orange flames and thick black smoke. The glass in the windows shattered when the explosion hit and glass rained down on the inside of our house.

"Hurry!" Uncle called from the living room. "The fire's heading for the side of the house! Hurry! It's gonna blow in a minute." I heard him hopping toward the front door on one foot, banging into the living room furniture as he went.

I dashed through the kitchen and slipped onto the back porch. The screened-in room was filled with smoke. Thick, flickering orange flames engulfed the backyard. I started coughing and fought my way over to the motorbike. The key was in the ignition. I sat in the saddle and kicked up the kickstand. I had watched Uncle Harry start the bike. I had sat on the porch and studied the stuff he had told me about starting and driving the bike. But it was a machine. And machines were my worst enemy.

Kick hard. Give it some throttle. Then rev her up. Lots of leg in the kick. I stomped on the kick-starter with all my might. The motorbike made an umph-umph sound and died. I tried it again. Same thing.

I felt the heat from the blaze on my face.

I tried to kick start the bike again. Umph-umph. Dead.

Another explosion rocked the building. The walking oil had turned into the flaming oil and had hit the side of the house with a vengeance. The crash of dishes shattering in the kitchen added to the uproar.

A rush of strength went straight to my leg as I plunged down on the kick-starter. Umph-umph . . . Umph-umph-umph-umph-umph. I twisted the throttle. Umph-umph-umph. The motorbike came alive.

Gears. I had to shift the gears. Pull in the clutch. One down with my foot. The thing on the left. That's what Uncle Harry said. One down. Then two up. First things first. Clutch. Then a little throttle. Then one down. Click. Ease up with a little gas.

The motorbike lunged across the porch, crashing into the wicker table. I turned the handlebars. The bike tipped over. The back tire skidded around. I eased off the gas. The bike bucked. I jerked the handlebars up, straightened myself in the saddle, took a deep breath, and tried again.

Clutch, shift, more gas. Then suddenly the bike and I rocketed into the kitchen, banging into the counter and then rebounding into the kitchen table. The tires crunched over the broken dishes. A flat tire? Too late to worry about that. Ease the gearshift lever up. More gas.

The motorcycle crashed into the living room. A solid mass of flame consumed the right wall. The smoke was so thick I could barely see Uncle Harry crouching by the door. The living room felt like the inside of an oven. The drapes were fences of fire.

A little more gas. The bike bucked forward.

Uncle Harry hopped over to the front door and threw it open.

The bike jerked and lurched up beside him. Using both hands, Uncle Harry struggled to raise his injured leg. Finally, he eased it over the saddle and thumped down behind me in the seat, wrapping his arms tight around my waist. "Let 'er rip!" he yelled over the roar of the engine and crackling flames.

And I let 'er rip. Lots of gas. One gear down and two up. The motorbike leaped forward out the open front door, banging over the threshold. The tires slid to the left. I forced them back in a straight line. I heard something explode behind us. No time to look back. More gas. The motorbike jumped forward.

A sheet of flame where the walking oil had ignited covered the walkway in front of the house.

Uncle Harry put his mouth close to my ear. "Run it!" he yelled. "It's our only chance. Fast as you can." His grip tightened around my middle.

I hunched over the handlebars and turned the right hand throttle as far back as it would go. I turned it back until my wrist ached. I gritted my teeth, lowered my head, and squeezed my eyes shut.

The engine bellowed and shook and vibrated and the motorbike rocketed forward—right into the billowing wall of fire.

≪ 24 ≫

The motorbike sped through the wall of fire so fast the flames didn't touch us.

Then things got crazy.

I heard the Indians yelling as we pulled away. I crunched down over the handlebars waiting for the Germans to open fire, but they never did. The motorbike was another matter. It lurched and pulled to the left and then to the right. Before I could straighten it out, we careened up on someone's front yard, hit a tire swing, and then crashed through a picket fence.

The bike had a mind of its own. It wanted to go left and I had to jerk it back to the right. I wrestled with the handlebars, twisting and turning them until I got us back on the street and headed for the Club.

Every time we hit a pothole or a bump, Uncle Harry let out a moan. His bandage came unraveled and trailed behind us along with the blood that came gushing out of his leg.

I got the bike into third gear, got the hang of steering the thing, and we sailed down the dirt roads of the Creole Camp. Hunched over the handlebars, I gripped them so tight my hands ached. I was determined not to let the motorbike turn over.

The wind slapped me in the face and the houses and company buildings flew past me in a blur. I opened the throttle full out, and we roared through the smoke from the burning camp buildings.

When I sputtered to a stop in front of the Club, John Long and a couple of other men leaped off the verandah. They sprinted to the street to help Uncle Harry. One of them helped me bring the bike to a full stop before I cut the engine. It was a good thing too because I couldn't do another thing. I slumped over the handle bars. One of the men lifted me from the motorbike and supported my weight as I staggered into the club.

Inside the Club, we got a real hero's welcome. People applauded and patted me on the back as the man led me to a chair. Someone handed me a bottle of Coca-Cola.

Mama hugged me and Uncle Harry again and again. She was so relieved she forgot to be mad at me for disobeying her. At least for that moment . . .

The Germans and their Indian allies continued their siege on the Club. Luckily the company men had lots of guns and ammo and kept up a steady fire from the roof and the windows in the bar.

"I can't believe what you did." Sonny Cole pulled up a chair and joined me at the table across from the entrance to the bar. He helped himself to the Coca-Cola another of my mamma's friends had just brought me. The Great Room was busier than an anthill. People packed sandbags around the windows and shuffled ammo to the men on the roof. Some folks just wandered around because they were too nervous to sit still.

"I didn't know it was gonna be so bad. Bullets and arrows. It's not like the movies," I said.

"If you say so," Sonny said. "But you sure are the cat's pajamas around here." His voice oozed with envy.

Over Sonny's shoulder I watched a couple of company men shove two tables together in the bar. One of them covered the table with a blanket. In a minute two other men hoisted Uncle Harry up on the makeshift bed. Blood gushed out of Uncle Harry's wound and pooled on the bar floor.

I began to collapse inside myself. Fire, arrows, gunshots, blood, and more blood. It was too much. I felt sick and dizzy. My hands shook so much my soda spilled.

"I was with the other men on the roof," Sonny said. "They shot a couple of the Krauts. Killed 'em dead in the street in front of the company store. Couple of Indians too. You don't need to worry. The company men will keep us safe."

"I'm not worried," I said, trying to pull myself together. I didn't want to lose it in front of Sonny, but I could not control my trembling.

The men in the bar set up two more makeshift beds. The door that led to the roof opened and some of the men helped Dorsey and another fellow into the bar and lifted them up on the tables. Dorsey's arm was bleeding and the other man held a crimson-soaked towel to his neck.

This wasn't the way life was supposed to be. Life

was supposed to be baseball and comics and quiet walks in the woods with Hannah. Kisses in the pantry. Not all this blood and pain and sorrow. I could feel the Shadow of Death hovering over the Club. My gut went cold.

Sonny turned around and followed my glance. "I was on the roof when they got hit. I don't think it's too bad."

I nodded, wondering who he was trying to convince—me or himself.

All around us the women of the camp scurried around, herding small children away from the windows, talking to each other in hushed tones. Back in the corner, Mrs. Sullards led a group of little kids in a singsong to keep them calm. The strains of "The Farmer in the Dell" filled the Great Room.

"I'm gonna join the Navy, soon as I'm old enough," Sonny said. "I ain't scared of the Germans or the Japs."

I guess Sonny was just scared of tarantulas.

Back in the bar, Dorsey and the other man were stretched out on the tables with blankets under their heads like pillows. The doctor from the company infirmary was looking after them. A cigarette dangled from the side of his mouth. He had on greasy-looking green corduroy trousers and a rumbled white shirt with his tie pulled down. He needed a shave.

The doctor slapped a bandage on Dorsey's arm and wrapped some gauze around the wound. Then he handed Dorsey a half-filled bottle of whiskey. Dorsey grinned and took a generous swig from the bottle.

"I hear the men on the rig drove the Indians back again." Sonny scratched the side of his face.

"My dad went out there early this morning," I said.

"My dad and some other fellows are guarding the administration building."

The doctor put a bandage on the other wounded man's neck and passed him the whiskey bottle. The man took a swig and wiped his mouth with the back of his hand.

"The company's gonna ship all of us back to the states," Sonny said. "All the women and children. They want the men to stay here and work on the rigs."

I wondered how Mama would feel about that. She hated the camp, but I didn't think she'd like being separated from Daddy. But our country was at war and I guess lots of families were about to get torn apart.

"They're gonna close the school," Sonny said in an oddly detached voice.

"Fine by me," I said.

Sonny barely managed a smile.

When I looked back over Sonny's shoulder into the bar, the doctor was talking to Uncle Harry. Uncle Harry's skin was pale and he had trouble sitting up. The doctor wrapped a new bandage around Uncle Harry's leg and tossed the old blood-soaked bandage into a grocery bag. Then he fished around in his pants pocket and pulled out a tiny medicine bottle. He kept the bottle cupped in his hand as if he wanted no one to see it while he shook out a couple of white pills. He looked around the room. When he was sure no one was looking, he bent over and stuck the tablets into Uncle

Harry's mouth.

Uncle Harry chewed up the pills.

"I'll be glad to get home to Louisiana," Sonny said. "I've had all the Venezuelans and Germans I want."

The doctor lifted Uncle Harry's head and gave him a drink from the whiskey bottle. Then he looked around the room again.

Sonny just kept on talking.

I spent the afternoon helping the company men stack sandbags on the roof. It was better than sitting around the Club, nerves on edge, listening to Sonny Cole going on and on about nothing. Around dusk, the gunfire died down and things got quiet.

"I think they're gone," one of the men on the roof said. "I think they've gone back into the jungle."

Another man pushed his sweat-stained hat on the back of his head and lit a hand-rolled cigarette. "Johnny Long says the Marines will be here tomorrow. Then we'll teach the Krauts a lesson if they come back."

"Amen, brother."

I caught up with Mama who had been helping the other ladies make bandages. We went into the bar and talked to Uncle Harry.

"You saved my life, son," Uncle Harry said quietly. The pills had improved his color and he was sitting up.

I didn't know what to say.

"I owe you one. You too, Dixie. Your boy is one courageous young man."

Mama gave Uncle Harry an awkward hug.

"Have Ches stop by when he gets back," Uncle Harry said. "I want to hear what happened out on the rig. I wish to God I'd been out there with him and the fellows." Talking made Uncle Harry break out in a coughing fit.

Mama wiped the sweat off his forehead with a handkerchief. "Don't talk anymore now," she said. "You rest. We'll come back and see you later."

Uncle Harry nodded and rested his head on the stack of blankets that served as a pillow.

Mama and some of the other women went into the Club's kitchen and made a stack of bologna sandwiches. When they ran out of bologna, they made peanut butter and jelly sandwiches. Everybody grabbed a sandwich and sprawled in the Great Room for an impromptu picnic. We all listened for the gunfire to start again, but the night stayed quiet.

After some discussion, we all decided to spend the night at the Club and wait for the American Marines to come the next day. John Long led us in prayer.

It was hot and stuffy in the Great Room and Mama and several other people decided to sleep on the roof. There had been no sign of the Indians or the Germans for six or seven hours and everybody assumed sleeping on the roof would be safe. A couple of company men volunteered to stand guard.

Mama and I picked out a spot behind the shed where the door from downstairs was located. We hauled up some cushions from the sofas in the Great Room, found a couple of blankets, and made a pair of comfortable beds behind the shed.

I thought I'd be too excited to sleep—I had driven a motorbike through a wall of flame that morning—and I tossed and turned for a few minutes, listening to the sounds of the night creatures, looking at the stars, and thinking about Hannah.

I must have drifted off to sleep because the next thing I knew I woke up with a start and saw Mama hunkered down by the west wall of the roof, deep in conversation with John Long. I tried but there was no way I could go back to sleep.

When Mama came back, I saw her face in the moonlight and I knew something awful had happened. Her eyes were rimmed with fresh crying. I sat up and Mama threw her arms around me and held me close in a way that she hadn't done since I was a little boy back in El Dorado.

"I need to talk to you," Mama said as she sat down on the sofa cushions. Her voice sounded flat and lifeless.

"Yes, ma'am."

"John Long just told me your daddy was right. The attack on the camp was nothing but a diversion. The Germans wanted to destroy the oil rigs and prevent the Americans from using the oil for the war."

"Daddy's usually right about that kind of thing," I said.

Mama nodded. "German sailors and Indians hit the rigs hard. John Long said the battle went on most of the day." Mama took a deep breath, exhaled, and looked at the moon for a while.

I rested my arms on my knees. Part of me couldn't wait to hear whatever Mama was gonna say and part of me wished I never had to hear it.

"The company men drove the Germans and the Indians back. They saved the oil rigs." Mama started twisting her wedding ring back and forth.

"That's great news," I said.

"Yes it is. The company men succeeded because the native workers fought side by side with them. They would never have done that if it hadn't been for your father." She paused and twisted the ring some more. "He always treated the workers with kindness and respect. Everyone was equal on the rig. That's why he was such a great drilling supervisor."

I opened my mouth but no words came out. A soul-chilling sense of dread seized me and held on tight. It felt like the worst thing ever in my life was about to happen, and there was nothing I could do to stop it.

"John Long said your father was like a great general today. He said your daddy organized everything, issued orders and fired his pistol with bravery when the attackers tried to get on the oil rig." Mama twisted the ring so hard I thought she might pull her finger off.

"A second ago you said Daddy 'was' a great drilling supervisor."

Mama sighed. "Yes I did. We're going to have to get used to that." Emotion came rushing back into her voice like lava pouring over the side of a volcano.

"Get used to it, since now it's just you and me in this horrible place. In this horrible war." Her voice cracked and she bit down hard on her lower lip.

I held my breath and braced myself like a bully was about to slug me in the face.

"Your daddy shot half a dozen attackers." Mama's whole body convulsed and her words came out in stops and starts. "Before . . . one . . . of the Germans . . . shot . . . him . . . dead in the heart."

‹‹ 25 ››

Like in the movies, the Marines arrived and everything was okay. Only it wasn't. Nothing was okay. The camp was safe and everybody left the Club and went home. The Marines patrolled the streets with rifles at the ready and handguns in holsters and we all knew the Germans wouldn't dare come back.

Since the Indians had burned down our house, Creole assigned Mama and me temporary quarters in the old English compound. We were supposed to live in this little house until the company could make arrangements to ship us back to the states. The house was dusty and full of mismatched furniture and Mama and I didn't have any interest in turning it into a home. It was just a place to eat and sleep.

The women from the Club conducted a drive and dropped a box of donated clothes on the front porch. The best thing in the box was an old checked shirt that had belonged to Robby Snedden. I'd seen Robby wear the shirt and I thought it was uglier than the dog's butt, but it fit and I was glad to have it.

Uncle Harry went back into the hospital. Mama told me he wasn't doing so hot.

That was one of the few things she said to me. Mama had run out of words. Daddy's death had taken her spirit. She stumbled through the days like a zombie.

I didn't have many words either. Daddy being dead didn't seem real to me. It seemed like a movie or a comic. It just wasn't real. I kept thinking Daddy would walk through the door with his hat cocked back on his head and his pipe in his mouth and ask what was for supper.

A couple of days after we moved into the English compound, Mama made a cup of coffee and sat down at the kitchen table and stared out the window. She never picked up the cup. The coffee got cold and Mama stared and stared on into the morning.

I decided to leave her alone with her grief, so I slipped out of the house and took a walk.

Gunmetal clouds hovered low in the sky and the humidity generated a light sweat all over my body. The whole camp shimmered with damp heat. Robby Snedden's shirt clung to my back like an angry leech.

I wandered around for a while and then drifted over to our old neighborhood. Along the way I ran into a couple of Marines. Their uniforms were crisp and they had rifles over their shoulders. They didn't look that much older than me, but they looked strong and tough.

The Marines smiled and nodded at me. I nodded back.

I wandered down our old street until I came to the burnt shell that used to be our house. The walls in the front had collapsed but the ones in the back were still standing. Everything was charred black.

I drifted into what used to be our living room. Mama's phonograph had collapsed into a heap of ashes. So much for the Andrew Sisters and Glenn Miller. There were piles of debris and black lumps where our furniture used to be.

In the back of the house, I was surprised to see that my old room was still okay. Sorta. A fine coating of ashes covered the bed, the dresser, and the nightstand and the floor was a sea of dust and ashes. A heavy burnt smell filled the air.

I crunched across the ashes and crud on the floor and opened the drawer of my nightstand. Dust flew everywhere. But inside the drawer, my comics were fine. They were in a neat stack, held together by a rubber band, like they were waiting for me. I scooped them out of the drawer and ran my hand over the cover on the top. *Superman*. Nothing could destroy Superman. I clutched the comics to my chest like I was embracing an old friend.

I thought about my dad. About how bad I had felt that day in the hospital when I yelled at him about bringing our family down here. I yelled at him when his hand was hurt. That was a crappy thing to do and I felt awful about it.

But Daddy made everything okay. Just like he always did. That night in the kitchen he told me I could come and talk to him any time. I never did, and standing in the rubble of our house, I wished with all my might that I had. Now I really needed to talk to him. Only now it was too late.

I poked around in the rubble for a while but didn't

find anything worth keeping. I finally gave up my search and wandered back down the street toward our new home in the English compound. We hadn't lived in the old house long enough for me to get attached to it, but seeing the charred shell of the house still had a big effect on me.

As I walked away, I realized that the house was a building and nothing more. What had been in the house was stuff. Stuff that could always be replaced. What couldn't be replaced was the people I had lost. My dad and Hannah.

You could always get a new photograph or some new shirts but you could never get another dad. Or another girl like Hannah.

As I wandered back down the street, I considered walking over to the German compound, kicking open the door of Hannah's house, going in, and finding her figurines and cherry wood box.

But that was just stuff. That wasn't Hannah.

After that I felt an emotional numbness attacking me like a case of the flu. I didn't want to think about Daddy or Hannah or the war or any of it anymore.

But you can't hide forever.

A week later, Mama and I boarded a freighter out of Maracaibo bound for New Orleans. We were heading home to El Dorado.

The freighter sailed under the name *Morning Star* and was older, smaller, and chunkier than the ship that brought us to Venezuela. The first day out, Mama stayed in our cramped little cabin all day. I went up top and stood at the railing, smelling the salt air, watching the rolling whitecaps. It still hurt too much to think about Daddy or Hannah, so I thought about other stuff.

And that's when I figured out who killed Mr. Taggert.

The freighter's sick bay was located on the deck below our cabin. I had to step over thick cables and boxes to get to the door. Five company men had been injured in the attack on the camp and were heading stateside for medical treatment. The room was dark and hot and smelled like iodine and vomit. The five beds were crammed together in a tight row. Uncle Harry was in the last bed.

I pulled a wobbly folding chair next to him. He was lying on his back, staring at the ceiling. His tanned skin drooped from his skeletal frame like an old brown lunch sack. Veins stood out on his neck.

"They treatin' you okay?" I said. I had prepared myself for what I had to do, but my voice came out all quivery.

"I can't complain." Uncle Harry managed a weak smile. "Although that would be the first time. How's your Mama?"

"Sad in her soul."

Uncle Harry nodded. The effort brought beads of sweat to his forehead. His face was flushed, and I suspected he had a fever. He was a big man who filled up the whole bed and made the entire room seem even smaller than it was.

All the men in the room had IV tubes in their arms. The tubes ran back to bottles of medicine that hung from portable stands and hovered over the injured men like guardian angels. A couple of the men were asleep, their irregular snoring providing background music for the sickbay. The man in the bed near the door kept up a steady cough. It sounded like he wanted to bring up Lake Maracaibo out of his lungs.

"How you feeling?" I lowered my voice.

"Like somebody shot an arrow through my leg."

"Everybody says the Indians put poison on the arrowheads."

"That's what the doctors tell me."

"Stay strong, Uncle Harry," I said. "Once you get stateside, you'll have the best care money can buy."

"Don't bet the ranch on it. Creole will shove us into a warehouse somewhere with some medical school dropout in charge. We can't work anymore. The company can't use us anymore. You can bet we'll get the cheapest care possible."

At least Uncle Harry felt well enough to rail at the company.

I nodded. "I meant you'd have all that money you were winning at poker."

"Huh?"

"Back at the bachelor barracks."

Uncle Harry's body tensed.

"You'd been telling us how you were cleaning up at the poker table. You said taking the other fellows' money was like taking candy from a baby. I heard you say that a bunch of times."

"The cards were good to me," Uncle Harry said. "It happens. What of it?"

"That's not what Darcy and Slim told me," I said, drawing in a deep breath. I had let the genie out of the bottle and it was too late to put it back.

Uncle tried to sit up, but the pain in his leg forced him back down. He frowned at me.

"Darcy said Slim was the one with all the luck. They said you were the Washington Senators of poker."

Uncle Harry ran his hand over the stubble on his chin. His eyes wandered all over the room. He was trapped.

"Darcy said you're too greedy to be a good poker player."

"Darcy's got a big mouth." Uncle Harry clinched his fists and struggled to sit up again. He didn't make it.

"Maybe," I said. "But it sure seems strange that if you'd been losing at poker in the bachelor barracks and you lost some cash on the ferry ride over to Maracaibo and you lost more dough at the cockfights you still had enough to buy the motorbike."

"You're gettin' too big for your britches, boy."

"I'm growing up, Uncle Harry. It happens."

Uncle Harry grimaced. "Let's just drop the subject. It's old history."

"It was the guy at the cockfights, wasn't it?" I said, ignoring Uncle Harry's last comment. "The man with the big tennis bag. You sold him something, didn't you? Something that had been in your duffle bag."

Uncle Harry locked in on me with a fierce stare down. I ignored him.

"I saw you show him some little brown bottles. They looked like medicine bottles. Then you pulled something else out of your duffle bag. But the man made you put it back real quick. The more I thought about it, the more I realized you were probably showing him stuff from the hospital. The duffle bag was full of medical supplies, wasn't it?

"Now you're way out of line, junior." Uncle Harry was almost shouting. His breath stank like rotting turnips.

"You dumped everything in your duffle bag into the man's tennis bag when the two of you were hidden in the back of the cockfight ring. Didn't you? I didn't see that, but I'm willing to bet that's what happened."

"You'd lose that bet."

"I don't think so. I've been doing a lot of thinking lately and everything came together this morning. That was just part of it."

"You gonna tell me the rest, smart guy?"

The man in the first bed let out a series of barking coughs. I waited for the coughing to subside.

"For one thing, when Mama and Daddy and I came to visit you in the hospital after you took the arrow in your leg, you were out of your head, saying all kinds of crazy things. At least we thought they were crazy. You kept mumbling about sulfur and iodine and penicillin and pain pills. At first we thought those were just the medicines they were giving you."

"And then?"

"And then it occurred to me. Those were the medicines the company hospital had been running out of the last few months. But what really struck me as odd was the fact that you had a room in the hospital all to yourself. A lot of the other men who got hurt in the attack had to stay in beds out in the hospital hallway."

Uncle Harry's eyes swept the room like a caged animal looking for an escape route.

"You were getting all the medicines you needed. The other men weren't so lucky. Just like over at the Club after you and I had our wild motorcycle ride. The doctor slipped you pain pills while the other men got a shot of whiskey."

"Get outta here, Ricky. You've overstayed your welcome," Uncle Harry snarled. "And don't come back." Spittle flew out of his mouth and landed on my shirt.

I leaned back in the chair. "You see where I'm going with this, Uncle Harry. It's a pattern. When Daddy cut his hand on the rig, the doctor didn't have the right sutures. When Robby Snedden got hurt over at the school, the hospital didn't have anything to fight the infection."

Uncle Harry had a coughing fit of his own. I let it pass.

"A friend of mine told me her father thought there were thieves and men of no character in the camp," I said, remembering Hannah's letter.

Uncle Harry's face glowed red. He was bathed in sweat. He wiped his chin with the back of his hand.

"I saw you at the picnic table behind the bachelor

barracks. Talking to the doctor. I saw you two joking around at the movies on the tennis court. You and the doc were pretty thick. How'd it work, Uncle Harry? The doctor stole the medical supplies from the hospital and gave them to you and you sold them on the black market in Maracaibo?"

Uncle Harry's mouth hung open.

I wanted to wipe the sweat off my face but I was afraid to move. My mouth felt like it was stuffed with cotton. Everything was like a dream.

"You been reading too many of those comic books, kid." Uncle Harry's voice sounded raspy and wheezy.

"I'm close though, aren't I? There must be a huge market for that stuff in Maracaibo. My guess is health care in Venezuela is something out of the last century. Suddenly here comes this American with an unlimited supply of penicillin and sulfur drugs and sutures and Lord knows what else."

Uncle Harry gave me a look that belonged on a rattlesnake. "Okay, smart guy, what if I did do something like that?" He pointed a shaking finger at me. I wanted to back away but I held my ground. "The company owed me. Your father and I risked our lives on those rigs. We worked our tails off and they paid us peanuts. The Rockefellers eat caviar and drink French champagne while the likes of us have to get by on hot dogs and warm beer."

I heard the man in the next bed stirring.

Uncle Harry must have heard him too. He lowered his voice. "What if I did stick it to the company? The company can afford it. What if I did take a little extra for myself? So what?"

"Because that makes you a thief." Tears welled up in my eyes.

Uncle Harry let out a choked laugh. "I might have known Chester Parker's boy would turn out to be a self-righteous little do-gooder."

I shrugged. I was past Uncle Harry's words hurting me. I had ripped away Uncle Harry's mask and seen the demon underneath. The room grew hotter and the humidity and the sick-people smell crushed in on me. Uncle Harry's face dripped sweat, soaking the sheets.

"How could you do something like that?" I said. "Everybody trusted you. You were the great Uncle Harry." The heat and humidity in the sick bay closed in around me. The buzzing in my head got louder. Drawing a single breath was a struggle.

"Shut up! You hear me! I'm sick of all of you." Uncle Harry's face contorted in pain and rage as he twisted around on the bed. The veins in his neck throbbed. "You, Chester, Dixie. All of you." His voice rose several octaves. "You can't take company property, Harry. Everything belongs to the company." He was shouting, his eyes crazy-wide. "It's not for the likes of Harry Kramer. That's what that running dog lackey Taggert said. It all belongs to the company."

Uncle Harry's body convulsed with another coughing fit. This time blood flecked his teeth and lips. "All those drugs and medicines and bandages. Taggert said they all belonged to the company. It just wasn't right. He was gonna fire me. That's why I . . ."

That's when I knew I had been right. That's when I knew what had happened the night Hannah and I found the dead body in the pipe. I wanted to stop. To make everything go back like it used to be. I wanted to make Uncle Harry well again.

But Uncle Harry's mouth kept going. Right to the finish line.

《 27 》

That evening I took my comics up to the top deck, where I flopped down on a bench near the railing. I spent a few minutes watching the sun set and the whitecaps wash up against the side of the ship.

I thumbed through *Captain Marvel* and *Superman* and *Detective* comics. I'd read them so many times before I knew the stories by heart. They were great stories: heroic deeds; good guys defeating bad guys; justice victorious; honor and duty the order of the day.

Mama was on a crying jag and asked me to leave the cabin. So I had some time to kill. I hadn't told her about Uncle Harry and Mr. Taggert. There'd be time for that later. Now that I knew what had happened the whole thing seemed so simple.

Mr. Taggert had caught Uncle Harry selling the company's medical supplies on the black market in Maracaibo and threatened to fire him. Uncle Harry had chased Mr. Taggert down near the giant pipes and killed him with a knife while we were all getting ready to watch the movie on the tennis court. Then Uncle Harry came back to the movie and sat with the doctor and some of the other guys.

Uncle Harry had covered his tracks. He planted the story about the Germans having a secret radio to contact the U-boats in the Caribbean and Mr. Taggert finding the radio and the Germans murdering him before he blew the whistle on their treachery.

It was a great story. He knew the Germans had a radio and that gave them a great motive for murder. Then the Japanese attacked Pearl Harbor and the Molitones raided the oil rigs and everyone forgot about Mr. Taggert's murder.

Good plan, Uncle Harry.

Only I had connected the dots and Uncle Harry had lost his temper and spilled the beans about Mr. Taggert. That had left me in a weird place. I needed to tell somebody, but I didn't have any proof. No real evidence. We had all left Venezuela for good. We were in the middle of a war. What would the authorities do?

The funny thing was it didn't matter. Uncle Harry didn't know it, but he was dying. Just before we left the Creole Camp to go home, the doctor told Mama that the poison from the arrow had gotten into Uncle Harry's system and was eating up his liver. The doctor told Mama he'd be dead in a few months.

There was a weird justice in there somewhere.

The last rays of the sun warmed the deck. I closed my eyes and drank in the warmth. Uncle Harry. A thief and a murderer. The real world wasn't like the comics. Not even close.

One thing I knew for sure was that my father had been a war hero. There was no question in my mind that he had died with his pipe clinched tight in his mouth, his guns blazing away, defending his oil rig. Defending America's oil rig.

And there was no doubt in my mind that, someway, someday I would see Hannah Oudt again. All wars end eventually. And when this one ends, I might travel to Heidelberg and find Dr. Oudt's house and, I hope, Hannah.

And if not Heidelberg, maybe someday I would go back to Venezuela and see Angel Falls. I'd stand there watching the spectacular cascade, the water hurdling down from a dizzying height, and then spraying out in a million directions in a timeless repetition of the awesomeness of nature.

Off to the side, on a gravel path next to the waterfall, a beautiful woman would step out of the mist and smile at me, her freckled face as radiant as the sun. Hannah and I would be together again.

The rivers would never run dry.

The shadows of evening finally encompassed the deck of the *Morning Star*. The sound of the waves striking the side of the freighter provided the only sound in my reverie of hope.

That's what it was—hope. Hope that the war would end soon. Hope that Mama and I would get back to El Dorado and build a new life. Hope that I would see Hannah Oudt again.

But hope's a funny thing. It's easy when everything is going your way. You figure things will just keep on getting better and better. Your hitting streak will last forever.

Hope gets a lot harder when things start to going

bad. And then gets worse. But when that happens hope is your only ally. Your best friend. Hope is what will pull you out of your slump. Hope is what will make the tough times bearable. You have to lock arms with hope, hold your head up, and march into the future.

I got up off the bench and walked over to the ship's railing. The blue-gray ocean was calm and stretched as far as I could see. The salty air smelled clean and fresh. The sun had sunk below the horizon, the last golden rays giving the sky an orange tinge.

I leaned against the rail for a while and took it all in—Venezuela, Daddy's death, Hannah Oudt, the war, the future.

Then I flung all my comics over the railing into the sea.

THE END

ABOUT THE AUTHOR

Jim Lester grew up in Little Rock, Arkansas, and now lives in Denver, Colorado, where he hikes the Rockies, walks his cocker spaniel and hangs out with his beautiful wife. He is the author of several books including a YA novel entitled *Fallout*, which Booklist called "a fast paced, clever coming of age story-Salingeresque in spirit," another YA novel entitled *The Great Pretender*, which received consistently good reviews on Amazon, a book called *Greater Little Rock*, and a sports history book called *Hoop Crazy: College Basketball in the 1950s*. You can contact Jim at his Web site: www.JimLesterBooks.com.